# Hiam

Eva Sallis was born in Bendigo. She has an MA in literature and a PhD in comparative literature from The University of Adelaide. She lives near Port Adelaide.

# Hiam

## Eva Sallis

ALLEN & UNWIN

Quote on p 139 reproduced from the *Koran*, Sura al-Rahman.

First published in 1998 by
Allen & Unwin
9 Atchison Street, St Leonards 2065 Australia
Phone: (61 2) 8425 0100
Fax:     (61 2) 9906 2218
E-mail: frontdesk@allen-unwin.com.au
Web:    http://www.allen-unwin.com.au

National Library of Australia
Cataloguing-in-Publication entry:

Sallis, E. K. (Eva K.)
  Hiam.

  ISBN 1 86448 676 7.

  I. Title.

A823.3

Set in 10/15pt Palatino by DOCUPRO, Sydney
Printed and bound by Australian Print Group, Maryborough, Victoria

10 9 8 7 6 5 4 3 2 1

# Acknowledgements

I would like to thank my publisher Sophie Cunningham, my inhouse editor Annette Barlow and Allen & Unwin's publicity director Monica Joyce, who together made the experience a great pleasure.

I would also like to thank my editor and proofreader Dite Wilde who straightened *Hiam* out before anyone else saw it.

Finally, I would like to thank Roger who has been part of everything that went into writing this book.

for TMW

As she headed beyond the confines of the known outer suburbs and beyond Mallala, the home of the furthest visited relative, she was ejected from her familiar Australia into a vast, monochromatic land, stitched up with patchy fences, overlaid with weedy paddocks, stubbly paddocks, golds, browns, and more subtle browns. The broken stalks of some rusty-coloured plant stuck up untidily from the bare allotments. Some of them were filled with rusty rolls of wire and dilapidated machinery. None of it was empty enough to be desolate but it was all the worse for that. The joyless and scrambled buildings and the wilting horses on grassless paddocks made it seem emptier than desolation. It was new and it was ugly. Even the dull leaves of the exhausted trees seemed brown. The car roared, the wheels grinding into the road with an inexhaustible energy, the engine shaking her through the thighs and buttocks, soothing, mind-numbing, leading and accompanying her into the unknown.

The land began to undulate after a while and

became increasingly more golden and disturbing. Beautiful colours crept in and were spread through larger and larger paddocks until the fences ceased to be an important part of the picture. At some indefinable point it made the transition from the miserable to the faintly glorious. Pale gold fields rolled from the highway to the horizon, meeting the blue sky in muted splendour. Even the fence posts in the foreground didn't stand out, being of some weathered, silky-grained, silver timber. Sometimes the light breezes ruffled the expanse in waves, making the grasses reflective and glossy like the rich pelt of some exotic and healthy animal. Something stirred and stared out from within her. She didn't want to see anything like this. She started to tremble and forced herself to focus on the colours of the steel-blue road ahead.

She passed a lone hovel. It was near the road in a field of pale glistening gold. Its sandstone pieces were weathered and prominent, its roof mere ribs and shreds of grey hessian, the door gone, and a single window black, a wail with no voice. It reminded her of something but she couldn't think what. The richly coloured corn, the glistening fields and the empty ruin lingered like perfume in her mind until it faded and became as distant as a forgotten chant.

Nothing seemed real. She passed a pink lake. Monochromatically fairy-floss pink, with a small, iridescent centre; a shallow disc of pink water surrounded by the flat expanse of its rosy shores. It shimmered at her in a sea of bright grasses stretching to an undulating horizon. It held for a moment and then vanished, but when she looked out to the right again, there it was, hovering and passing; an Unidentified Earth Object. It was a different one, after all. It had clumsy, pretend monsters in it, near the road, made from half loops of car tyres. Had they been living, they would have been less strange. One of them carried some Christmas tinsel around its neck, gaily. Then the lake was gone, with its monsters, into the past and she didn't see another one.

She drove in a form of blank shock that she had actually left, severed the connection with people, family, pain. She was outside or more outside of something she had been in (which had also been an exile from something else). She was even slightly exhilarated. Whenever she thought that it was all the same and gained a jaded certainty about the world, it changed utterly, as the car shot away from any sense of familiarity, no matter how newly acquired. She was just getting impervious to the ripples and the impact of the wheatfields when she became aware of a mountain range rising ahead, tawny as a lion's head. She passed with it on her right as its colour deepened to a rich red-gold in the fading day, staining the long range and tingeing everything. Red and gold tips and crags in the pure and luminous sky. Nearer the road the bluish bushes picked up odd hues in the peculiar light. The range became endless and familiar but showed just enough of its hinterland and its dimensions to suggest it had breadth and secrets. She felt it looming between her and the open horizons of before. She stared at her hands. They seemed unfamiliar on the wheel. Strange that she had known them all her life but they were so odd now. She was veering unsteadily on the highway. She tried to think herself back into the long past, into a more solid-seeming world. Somehow she had brought few memories with her into the cocoon of the speeding car, scattered images and voices only. She tried to think back before Australia but she had no memories so far back, only facts. She sought out and embellished some memories from the early years as a charm against her rising panic. Don't think. Don't remember.

The water is soft and warm, slipping and rolling over her hands. The foamy water washes off the contours of her palms and through the crevices of her fingers like a spent wave receding from rocks. Her glistening hands lift, roll and plunge, expert without guidance. The dishes rise pristine from the suds. Hiam washes meditatively, soothed by the immersion and the mindless activity. Looking through the window, past the jumbled glass adornments and late, white roses

4

on the sill, she watches her small daughter Zena digging out in the yard.

The garden has suffered and the lawn is gone. The digging game has lasted almost six months and the flat, green expanse has been replaced by a small war zone, as if shelled into oblivion. Mounds and swellings and raw earth wounds stretch as far as the vegetable garden. Along the edges sunflower heads lie crushed face down on the ground, their broken and torn stalks like broken bones drying in the autumn air. Zena, a small determined mole, is playing blindly for the one correct hole.

Digging to Palestine had become a craze amongst six-year-olds that year. Forbidden from destroying their own backyards, kids had flocked to the Sherriff site. Zena permitted assistance, provided the destination was Palestine, and a small team possessing extraordinary endurance had arrived after school every day for ages. The yard is periodically dotted with little coloured backs and bottoms, hardworking soldiers, disciplined by Zena. Three kinds of digging tool are permitted; soft bottle caps, hard bottle caps with teeth, and found objects. Hiam experiences a mixture of wonder, pride and fear when she thinks about it. The entire yard has been rearranged capful by capful.

The ultimate prize is the destination but there are many rewards along the way. Beside the outside toilet The Through Earth Exploration Museum has been set up, filled with carefully arranged coins, shells, worn pieces of glass, rusty bolts, nails and tools, and bones.

As with wars, Hiam thinks and hopes that the rigours of winter will end the game; and in any case she is going to hide all harddiggers and softdiggers next spring.

Harddiggers with teeth, or beer-bottle tops, can scrape through rock. When Hiam went out that morning to hang the washing she had found herself looking down a roundish hole, three feet wide and three feet deep, carved through meticulously chewed rock. She felt slightly scared of her daughter. What monster could create such marks? She couldn't stop laughing.

Later that night she and Masoud are standing around the hole, shining the torch over its finely scored sides, laughing at their daughter's great work. It is a labour of love for her father. He catches his breath, staring into Hiam's eyes with a twisted smile and pale lips.

'Hiam, *I* have never even seen Palestine.'

She laughs. 'Better dig then,' she says softly, gently. She glances at him cautiously.

She was becoming tired. The slight exhilaration had long dropped away, leaving her shaken by the car, stiff from the imperceptible tension that had held all her muscles together, and vaguely aware that she had only staved off her nightmare by chance and circumstance. She felt fragile to the tips of her hair. Every moment of the past eleven weeks had struck her with the same thought. *Now*, right *now*, she was alone for the first time.

She didn't know where she was going, or why. It hadn't been important when she had started the car. Cushioned in a conscious, concentrated effort not to think, she had feverishly and methodically packed What One Might Need. She had settled into the sheepskin covered seat, mindful not to think, smoothly inserted the familiar key in the ignition, turned, revved, waved, driven off. She had completed these motions like a dancer in a ballet. Flawlessly, gracefully. She had concentrated on engine noises, tarmac feelings, rubber on road frictions, dusty consoles and the smell of Armorall. That was all a long time ago. Hours. She pulled over onto the gravel and stopped, staring out of the windshield. There was nothing to do, nowhere to go, nothing to be. She focused through the glass onto the ground ahead. There was a dead kangaroo on the steel-grey gravel, much larger than she had ever imagined them to be. Its fur was reddish, matted and bloody, the ground stained all around it. Its deformed looking hands were clasped together, strange legs stretched out away from its body in a disturbingly human repose. The enormous corpse filled her vision. Her pulse picked up speed and raced into thumping agony. Stopping was worse than going, that was all. She decided to drive to the next big town and then see. She pulled out onto the highway, heart leaping sickly in her chest, sweating and gasping again at the edge of her darkness. She clung to the steering wheel, staring ahead, foot to the floor. Going was better than stopping.

She tried to concentrate on the thin threads of the story. The story all happened a long time ago, all more than eleven weeks ago. It had a map and reasons. It was broad, meandering, populated and sane. Voices, houses, faces, clothes, colours, arguments, food. Masoud was lurking in the borders of her story. She could not look directly at him. Herself and Zena were easy enough to fashion from her memories, dreams and suppositions. Masoud hovered. It was easier not to know him, not to show him. It was easier not to have known him. She tried to let Masoud in only in the earliest or the happiest moments, and then the memory was muffled and bandaged and could speak only indistinctly.

She is eyelash to eyelash with Masoud, the side of her face touching the side of his face, bone to bone, looking sideways in, seeing dimly looming the mysterious regard of his eye. He says,

'Hiam, if you marry me, I will teach you to ride,' and they both laugh.

'Masoud, if you marry me, I will teach you to fall.'

'Hiam, if you marry me, I will rise again.'

'Masoud, if you marry me . . .' And she cannot think of a fitting retort. They laugh, kneeling in their embrace in the sun by his grazing horse.

If you marry me, what will I teach you, beautiful man? To be wild and free like me.

It was nearly dusk when she came to a large town. She crossed a long causeway streaked with slags of discoloured foam blown from the left-hand side, which was spread with a quiet salt inlet, broad and reflective, coloured grey, sprinkled evenly with tints of gold on its wavelets and deep slate blue. Over her right shoulder, however, chunks of white, glittering foam floated gaily away upon a rose-pink ocean, picking out some gold and red from the sky but unmistakably the same pale, uniform pink of the lakes before. It stretched away, pink as pink to its shores. There were people on the shores who paid it no attention. She filled up at a service station, proffering the money without speaking, accepting the change with a nod, then stopped at Hungry Jack's, feeling stiff and sore. She went in and ate very slowly, trying to think about the food and nothing else.

As she finished she thought of finding a hotel but felt so overcome with uncertainty and a sense of the insuperable difficulty of speaking to someone, let alone organising everything in the foreign and rapidly darkening town that she longed for the car, with its familiar smell and her things. She went eagerly back to the car and sat in it. She felt relieved but very far from home. She couldn't think of anyone she knew ever having even mentioned Port Augusta.

Hiam and Masoud stand looking into their house with the scarred and pockmarked yard yawning dimly in the falling darkness behind them. It is not a grand house. At the back it has a porch, asymmetrical windows and an amateur extension of gyprock board. The concrete of the porch isn't level and has water and mould marks where the water pools in winter. The plumbing clambers up the back of the house as if it has had to search for its entry holes in the wall. A small loquat tree shades one corner. Officially it drinks the laundry water, but it has begun to take a bit on the side from the drains. It is a plain, Australian house but slowly they are fitting into it. It is easier for Hiam.

She has moved several times in her life. It has

neither been a tragedy nor even a struggle. It has happened to her and, in her own way, she has enjoyed it. Each zone of her life is cordoned off into its own particular geography. Her early childhood is flooded with a sunshine of another earth. Her father's voice, the vines and orchards in the high, terraced mountains of the Yemen, the smell of crusty bread in the morning, and paintings traced in fine, black lines onto her arms and feet. Memories as faint and lingering as a smell of grandmother's hair, filling the vistas of a childhood felt more than remembered in images. The next phase is elsewhere. School in the bustling town in Jordan, in mother country, skirting the dogs, roaming around cheeky on Thursdays, springtime and almond blossom, sulking outside, back against the hot sandstone. University in Amman. The metropolis, people from everywhere, study guilt, friends and arrogance. Marriage, birth, emigration. It seems quite appropriate that life with Zena and Masoud meant a place completely different. Adelaide, her brother-in-law's house, then this house, *our house*. Most of the time Hiam feels very proud of it. They stand looking in. The light from the living room glows from the interior into the hall, past the bend, out through the kitchen, out through the open back door and, having found their still forms, illuminates them. Soft silhouettes of pot plants stand on the back porch. On the opposite side to the warm light of the living room is a warm darkness. To the left of centre their daughter lies asleep, breathing into the night

11

air. Hiam breathes in deeply and sighs. Masoud could be happy here. But everything is much harder for men.

She couldn't stay indefinitely in a car park, so she drove on up the road between rows of trees, reddish-brown in the dying light, up a rise to a roundabout, a divergence. At her right a road headed into unlit bush and out of sight and spontaneously she headed out into the intensifying darkness. The trees on either side became darker, dimmer and more fluid. Her foot stayed steady on the accelerator but her spirit quailed as she glanced from side to side. She should not be here. She could feel a mounting pressure at the back of her skull, a prescient, swelling fear. She could feel that this was the worst thing under the circumstances that she could be doing but, as if disconnected from the rest of her, her foot stayed steady on the accelerator. Darkness was suddenly so total that it seemed as if a cloud of smothering ash had buried the world. Her lights picked out the contorted shapes of road-side trees and shrubs in faded greys and yellows.

Something did happen.

The massive form of a kangaroo shot athletically over her bonnet and off into the darkness over her right shoulder, as if flying over the earth rather than leaping. It appeared in the lights high above the car and rushed with impossible speed obliquely towards her, darkening to a black silhouette in a split second. She saw its face, even its expression, but was shocked and shaken. Long after, she wondered if it did not really have dead eyes and blood-matted fur. She shook uncontrollably in the seat but her foot stayed steady.

Hiam, Jamila and Fatima are sitting around the stone table on Fatima's front balcony. Hiam is fingering the grey stone, soaking up the early warmth like a lizard. It is a lazy day, a clear morning of sun-soaking enjoyment of life at no pace at all. All three of them have planned for this morning's shared laziness. Indulgences lie waiting around them. The best fresh bread in Adelaide steams gently into the crisp air, its aroma recalling the best breads of three lifetimes. A smell of rich, cardamom-scented coffee meanders from the coffee pot. The silver sugar bowl rests inert, but Hiam knows that it has a vanilla bean buried in its belly, lying there like a secret. Perfect yoghurt from Gaganis Brothers, cheeses cut in geometric forms arranged on a blue tile like an artist's painting, rose-water-scented cheese skeins in a bowl drowned in syrup, and pistachio-filled squares of nougat and fudge are laid on the table. The iridescent parrots shriek gaily in the high tops of the eucalyptus trees, their three children shriek more viciously on the immaculate lawn, and incandescent sunlight streams down onto the last vapours of the dew from an intensely blue sky. A sense of wellbeing floods through Hiam's body and she stretches out her legs, kicking off her sandals and rubbing her soles against the cool, sculptured stone in the shade underneath the table. The two faces across from her look like a mirror. She can see in their faces the expectancy which none of them feel the need to satisfy. The breakfast day will be over all too soon and no part needs fulfilment right now.

Fatima is gazing without focus at her young son. Even when she is not concentrating there is a purposefulness in the unwavering direction of her attention. When Fatima appears to be meditating or praying, she is in fact scrutinising her son's opaque future for the unexpected. She has long ago planned for several versions of the expected. It isn't that Fatima distrusts her mother or the Aunties: she wishes to extend the boundaries of their undeniable expertise into the realm of the prophetic. There is something fixed and rocklike in Fatima's personality, both soothing and irritating.

Fatima is often asked to keep people company when they go to doctors or headmistresses, as she is able to act as a kind of interpreter. She knows exactly what emphasis to put on phrases like 'limited attention span', 'truancy', 'disruptive', 'reserved', 'behavioural disorder', 'criminal tendencies'. These

14

meetings are confrontational affairs in which families are insulted and humiliated with words and facial expressions which seem to mean more than they say.

Once, when Hiam answered the door she found Auntie Ilham standing outside dressed as if for a wedding in a white suit, pink lace and an elaborate hat. She sweeps in forcefully, her feathers quivering. 'Ya Fatima!', she calls out querulously, 'put on your best! We have to show them! We have to let those teachers know who they are dealing with!' The formidable woman is nearly crying with fear.

Hiam has learned gradually to fear schools and public institutions. It isn't that anything outright unpleasant ever happens. People are rarely as clear as that. It is simply the constant feeling of something unsaid and of meanings not granted by the understanding of words and it saps her strength because every reaction is inappropriate.

Zena, however, still reacts. When she was three, Zena slapped a doctor in the face for making Hiam cry. Hiam was crying because she didn't know why Rubella injections were a moral issue and she only guessed they might be from the doctor's inexplicable but obvious disgust. Zena stood there shaking in rage on the table, her black eyes on fire, level with those of the doctor.

Jamila admires both of these slightly older women: Hiam for her brains and education, and Fatima for her standing in the community, and, as with everything she admires, she feels also jealous. Jamila wants to receive admiration far more than she wants to give it and candidly says so. She is beautiful and praised satisfyingly for it.

Jamila's heart is torn by strong desires. In one given day the desire for a white silk dress can become so strong that she feels sick with it. Her desire for recognition from Hiam is something she can taste in her mouth and Hiam's delighted laughter at her jokes is like water on a desert land.

Jamila's black eyes have long lashes and her hair and make-up are perfect. *She is a beautiful woman.* Fatima had acquired the look of a mother as soon as she married and long before she conceived. In this moment she has the look of a contented and wise mother. *She is a beautiful woman,* Hiam thinks again, feeling exactly the same all-embracing sense of what makes up a beautiful woman as she felt a moment before looking at Jamila. She surveys the lawn, feeling like a lioness, narrowing her eyes. Their three cubs, Zena, Amin and Nada, are beautiful cubs. At this moment Zena is waist deep in the fountain catching tadpoles and Amin, squatting on the marble flags in his cream waistcoat, is glancing up with laughing eyes and a hand over his mouth. Nada is shrieking and spinning in some wild, almost automated ecstasy probably about the state of Zena's pretty dress. The bunched taffeta is clutched ineffectually in one of Zena's hands, spreading around her like a crumpled Easter egg wrapper. She has one elbow high in the air. The other arm is in the water up to the shoulder.

Her body is taut and vibrant with the clumsy, loose-limbed grace of all baby animals. They are all dressed to impress their friends' mothers. Let the cubs play, she thinks regally and turns back to the day ahead.

'Do you know Amina?' Fatima asks. This is a way of saying 'The subject is . . . Amina.'

'She's Christian isn't she?'

'Yes, but she married a Druze.'

They all look at each other and laugh luxuriantly. They don't mind that Amina has married a Druze but the whiff of scandal is a pleasure. Hiam privately considers the gossip about who has married whom and how pretty or ugly the outsider is, rather stupid. Having married a Palestinian herself, she believes that with Zena she will be open-minded.

Jamila says musingly, 'He is a very handsome man, like a movie star.' This is her highest praise. She looks like a movie star too. Several people have said so, including Hiam. They gossip aimlessly about Amina and mixed marriages. Then Jamila hunches her shoulders forward and lowers the level of the gaze of her laughing eyes, gripping them with an intense, conspiratorial look.

'I heard,' she says softly, 'I heard that Ibrahim has married an Australian. Auntie Saida told me. They met at the University.'

They all look at each other like half-startled gazelles, interested as if hearing of a gory death which is also remote. They are eager for more so they can know the worst, protect themselves from the same fate and congratulate themselves on their smooth, unscarred, happy lives. They graze again.

'His poor parents,' murmurs Hiam.

'Poor him, too, the fool. The Australians have no heart and no morals. Their parents *encourage* them to be prostitutes. She will stay with him for a while, have his children, and then run away with the Television Repair Man and take his children with her. She only took him for his money and she has ruined a good man.' Jamila sits back with the look of an oracle who has spoken.

'But his family has no money.'

'You know the Australians: as soon as they know you are Arab, they think you have money.'

'And guns.'

'And good sex.'

They laugh. Jamila says, 'Well, that part is true.' They laugh again.

'Well, *that's* what a university education does for your children in this country.' Jamila glances furtively at Hiam. Hiam is alone among her friends in having gone to university, a fact which proves troublesome at times. If she had dyed her hair, worn the *hijab* again, gone vegetarian or committed suicide it would have been ultimately put down to her education. She laughs but Fatima's eyes flicker in fiery irritation. Fatima is very proud of her educated sister-in-law.

Hiam says mildly,

'They do grow up very ill-treated, you know. Just look at the billboards. How can they have self-respect when wherever they go there are images of women treated with no respect? And they all drink. It must be very difficult.'

Jamila snorts. 'They like it that way.'

Hiam is not going to argue with them for anything. Participation is far more enticing than righteousness and she is prepared to lie happily for the pleasure of their company. Privately she cannot share their view of Australians. She feels rather sorry for Australians. The mothers of the children who have dug up her yard are sweet, sad women. The fact that they lack pride and self-respect, don't dress themselves or their children well and eat bland food means little or nothing. For sure, these things have simple explanations. Besides, most of their husbands and even some of the wives drink alcohol. Certainly, Australians grow up with little guidance from parents who themselves had never learned how to parent, guide and protect a child. Certainly, women are very ill-treated by the Westerners. Yet, somehow, they seem to make do. Some of them even seem happy, especially the married ones with children. If she was to ask Jamila or Fatima: 'Have you now, or have you ever had, an Australian friend?' they would answer, 'Of course not!' with some indignation that she should suspect it. They have met the mothers of their children's playmates too. And, indeed, she couldn't say that she has any Australian friends either. Although she really likes, even perhaps loves, some of the children and some of the mothers, they never seem to become friends. She doesn't need them, and perhaps they somehow know it.

The first time someone asked her what it was like growing up as a woman she was so confused that she stared, her mind sidling away rapidly like a crab on the seafloor. She had wondered if she was being ridiculed, checking first outwards and then flickering inwards with self-doubt about her English. She murmured hesitantly, 'Well, I started as a girl.' The woman who had asked her lost her earnest look and wrestled with her own sea creatures. When the question had become a predictable component of encounters with Australians, she had learned that the salient feature was that she grew up in an Islamic country and that Islamic woman was not the same thing as woman. Islamic. *Islam* is a curious word, here.

Long ago. Her father is softly praising God at sunrise in their garden; at the sea while she plays; his low voice among the pine trees while she lies on her back, staring up, feeling overfull after lunch. She remembers her father praising God in his happiness, in his loneliness, with longing, with satisfaction, with annoyance, with secretiveness. Her memories of her father are a kaleidoscope in all the different voices of a father. She dresses him herself on Fridays. She winds his headcloth, straightens his *jambiya*, trails the beads over it and sends him off, perfect, down the road. Her father and God are one with the beautiful clothes, the sun, the hot seashore, the hawk in the sky, the cold night, the dank predawn, sunset, pregnant sheep, the drying well in summer, the stone-baked bread and the smell of dinner, and the delicious sleep and dreams. This is God's world which her mother loves, her father praises and in which she lives as surely as an animal sensing the solstice.

By some magic it has been transformed into a small black stone. 'You live inside *that*?' Australians ask, and, having put her inside it, then pity her.

She had not realised how strange Australians would be and how powerful their view of her would be. She had stopped speaking to people but earlier she had occasionally tried. She senses now that unless she says what they already think, their pity grows the more she speaks. She finds the words dead on her lips and the sound of things precious to her becoming weak and piping as she looks into eyes that think they know something else about her. She and her friends know one thing clearly: being Muslim is not highly thought of and Australia itself is.

'It must be wonderful for you to live in Australia!'


A man once asked Masoud his nationality. Masoud said: 'Palestinian!' The man shook his hand warmly and said,

'Oh! We are brothers—I am in the IRA!'

Masoud liked it but it annoyed Hiam.

Someone once said,

'You must have been very strong to break free and come here!'

Free is another word. The more the black pebble is cast, the more trapped and lonely she feels, the more she revisits her memories, the more Australians say she is free now.

No Arabic retort has any power here and she is mostly left speechless.

'Were you *mutilated* as a child?'

After that one she stopped trying to talk to Australians, mainly because she had not struck that compassionate face down.

*God alone knows everything.* She sometimes wonders why the world is so unwelcoming. The stages of her life have led her further and further away from her father and deeper and deeper into exile.

There was an enormous crash and she went blind with terror. Without thought she slammed her foot onto the brakes and locked up all four tyres. In slow motion the dull ribbon of the road, the earth siding, the black, looming shrubs and the sky spiralled elegantly around her. She spun, wringing the visible world like washing, and came to rest half off the road, lights pointing back the way she had come. It was still; the car had stalled. She switched the lights off and sat in the darkness, in her head a heavy, vestigial humming, and the buzz of blood settling after the interminable moan and vibration of the engine.

What had she hit? She waited blankly and then started the car, switched on the lights, and rolled cautiously in second gear back to the crash. Something black and even lay across the whole road. She stopped the car, got out and walked stiffly towards it in the beam of her headlights. Her legs made moving bands of black across the road.

She hadn't hit anything. A great, metal grid was embedded into the road, covering a pit. Either side of it a low and tumbledown fence stretched away in a straight line off out of sight. Her fear subsided and she laughed. A kangaroo had jumped over her car bonnet. It would jump both the fence and the grid, unless there was some mysterious magic in the combination which confounded its reason. Everything seemed mad—keep what in or out of what? The land around appeared to be a monotonous, wild and desolate nothing.

She drove on through the night, welcoming the jarring compound crash of the grids which appeared at irregular intervals. The idea that this endless land was fenced with these threads struck her as a phenomenal folly.

Jamila is making an obscene gesture with her forearm and Fatima is laughing, sipping her coffee. Jamila loves to talk about her husband's performance. She is very proud of him and cannot resist sharing her knowledge of his virility.

'*Every* night, just like that, all night.' Her arm, elbow in her groin, with its clenched fist raised like some pugilist, looks so unlike a penis that they all laugh. It is black and smooth and plump and looks, if anything, soft and ineffectual. Fatima is a more reserved person but she too smiles knowingly when they talk about sex. Hiam wonders why she will not talk about Masoud like this. Masoud is better unknown by her friends. In any case, she doesn't know how to say that some things about lovemaking bother her. Maybe they bother everyone, and Jamila is talking, and Fatima smiling as a form of bravado and pretence. Do their husbands too refuse to look into their faces when they make love? Have their husbands too settled into preferring to be behind the more anonymous buttocks and backs of their wives rather than embracing their personal, individual fronts? Maybe, paradoxically, her own back and buttocks are unique and intimately familiar to Masoud, and it is only to her that they are strange; only to her they might be anybody's. She can never ask, because

24

it is a question of no bravado, and gives too much away of both her own and Masoud's frailties.

Fatima suddenly leans across to her.

'Hiam. *Habibti*. I miss you, and Zena. Do you remember the lovely time we had when you were living here? How is the house? I heard that you had begun landscaping the back. Good on you.'

Hiam laughs. It is the first time she has thought of the Through Earth Exploration as 'landscaping'. She says, seriously,

'It should look lovely when it is finished.' Then, smiling at Fatima, she says to Jamila,

'Do you know what I and Fatima did once when we were living here?'

Fatima shakes her head in laughing, almost serious protest, and Jamila breathes,

'What!' in anticipation of a revelation.

Hiam and Fatima both know without having discussed it that Jamila is an enjoy-at-own-risk proposition, but Hiam goes on anyhow.

'We went into town, looking for white slacks, just like those, yours. We got hungry and started looking for a place to eat. We went downstairs where Fatima was sure there was a restaurant, and we found ourselves in . . . guess.'

'A pub!' shrieks Jamila in delight.

'Worse,' says Hiam in a low voice, infused with innuendo. Fatima buries her face in her hands.

'No,' whispers Jamila, her beautiful eyes wide, her pupils dilated.

Hiam sits back and says in thoroughly normal tones, rapidly, as in a child's chant,

'Before I go on you must swear to silence and secrecy to the grave in the Name of God.'

'By my life, Hiam. By the eyes of Nada, I swear. Was it a men's gambling club?'

'Worse,' says Hiam in a low and husky voice. Fatima lifts her head and stares significantly at Jamila.

Jamila shivers in delight and fear. Hiam says matter-of-factly,

'It was a brothel!'

'Oh Lord, Oh Lord! How do you know? What happened? What did you see?!'

'Nakedness, mainly. We didn't really get inside, only into the foyer. Actually, they were very nice. They gave us some water, and showed us out.' Hiam feels tired of the story.

'Not before I screamed!' says Fatima proudly, suddenly bursting with the experience, 'Oh Lord! How I screamed!'

*And fainted*, thinks Hiam. She can remember the gloomy, reddish light, orange lampshades and purple carpet. She can remember the naked girls with trays turning towards them, the thud as Fatima hit the floor and the solicitous gentlemen in crisp suits, looking strangely doll-like and sexless in their immaculate clothing. A man ordered a girl with pale pink nipples to get them a drink. Hiam said water and, next instant, the nipples were in front of her and a glass was being handed to her. She realised with shock that a man was kneeling beside Fatima and, although she knew straight away that he was only helping, her mind writhed in horror at the thought that Fatima might come round just then. She pushed him, muttering that she would do it. Fatima sat up foggily and screamed quietly once more, as if the faint had simply cut her short. Hiam stood up, stroking her shoulder, waiting apprehensively for her to recover. She turned and found herself staring at the nipples which were bouncing slightly next to her. They looked assured, yet delicate and exposed. She looked up at the girl, who was eyeing her with curiosity. She had red hair. She did not have the look of a degraded exploitee of a B-grade, Lebanese movie.

'Why do you . . . ?' Hiam whispers suddenly, hotly.

The girl sneers just slightly, curling a beautiful, purple lip.

'Why did you?' she answers curtly.

'We thought it was a restaurant,' Hiam murmurs with shame.

'That's OK,' the girl says kindly, raising a manicured hand and touching Hiam's hand lightly, 'and I do it to pay for my studies.' The nipple gyrates mesmerisingly, and the girl turns and strides away.

Hiam is profoundly shocked. Fatima comes to and they scuttle out. Fatima has seen her talking to the girl but she has seen Fatima unconscious at a man's feet in a brothel. They know they are both safe. She has never told Fatima what the girl said.

'Praise be to God that you were there,' says Fatima with a shudder. She too remembers.

'The *Shame!*' Jamila, clapping her hands, throws her exquisite head back. She is deeply impressed. 'You showed them what decent women think of them!' She clearly considers Fatima very courageous and principled. Jamila does not know that screaming can be involuntary.

Hiam changes the subject.

'*Ya* Jamila, Nada is looking very lovely.' It is time to indulge in the ritual of complimenting each other's children and parenting. They all turn to look at the children who are huddling together in a brightly coloured mass in the corner of the garden, staring eagerly down the road intermittently praising God at the tops of their voices. Jamila looks bewildered and raises an inquiring eyebrow to Hiam and Fatima.

Zena and Amin like cars not according to their make but according to their form. Utilities are their favourite and, along with vintage cars, earn the title of Cars of Islam. Convertibles are anything with a horse float, because that converts whatever car is towing it to Islam, no matter what the creed. Amin and Zena amuse themselves for hours in the back of the car, praising God when a Car of Islam is recognised. Recently Zena has begun to like F100s, and Amin curvy little cars, and the game has had to be stopped because of the religious wars in the back

28

seat. Now they are seconding Nada, who, having not yet learned discernment, has only picked up enough of the game to praise energetically all cars.

Zena is ill, her small body lapping up the attention feebly as it flails restlessly at the fever. Hiam watches her, sleeping and waking, guilt-ridden about the tadpole-catching in Fatima's fountain. Sick children scare her and Zena is very rarely ill. The pale face, the sweetish, unusual body smell, the dampness—all are frightening and repellent. They have the effect of making her hold tighter and wish she was elsewhere. She hates illness and incapacity in anyone. She watches Zena's face in sleep, noting the pallor around the nose, the curve of the resting lips, the shiny throat. It is only the flu but all the ladies are kind enough to tell her every terrible flu tale they know.

'It might be the flu . . . '
'God willing it is just the flu.'
'The flu kills children Every Day.'
'The only thing with the flu is onions,'
'under the pillow,'
'under the neck,'
'on the chest,'
'on the forehead.'
'*Verses of Restoration. Verses of Preservation.*'
'The only thing with the flu is a Recitation.'
'Don't be silly: it's a flu, not a death.'
'You must repeat "*Ya Salam*" 160 times to her.'
Delighted to be able to help, Aunties from every-

where ring to chat about flu horror stories and to give advice. Most agree that whatever their faults, Jewish doctors are best. Hiam sits by Zena's side telling her stories and arguing with her hallucinations in between arguments with the Aunties on the phone.

Zena stares up at Hiam with bright eyes, her frail arms twitching feebly on the doona. *Ya Salam, Ya Salam.* Zena talks quietly and ceaselessly.

'Why is your village called "Who Knows"?'

'It's a joke name. An Englishman once asked someone: "What is the name of this place?" The man said "*Man Yadri*", and the Englishman wrote it down on the map. Later, your grandfather noticed that all European maps called it Man Yadri and it became a joke. Children learned it from school and people used it affectionately, and of course we always said it was called Man Yadri to Europeans.'

'What was its name before?'

'That's the funny part: it was called *Ain al-Alim*, The Well of God.'

'Why?'

Hiam leans the back of her hand against the beaded cheek, tucking her in the quilt. She brushes the hair aside and says, rubbing noses,

'*Man yadri*, ya Zena.'

'Mum, there is a King of the Jann in that corner, hiding. He says *Chyse Chokka Chyse Chaw Chyse Chokka Chyse Chaw* very softly when you are here, but very loudly when you go out.'

30

'OK. I'll tell you a story about a King of the Jann who was punished.'

'Good,' Zena says loudly to the corner.

She had been driving in the dark for hours. Everything except the road was so formless and indistinct that it might have been scudding clouds. Far in the distance she could see some lights, seemingly somewhere below her, although the road was flat and straight. It was a long time before the lights formed themselves into a small village. But when they did, she was virtually upon it. It had a brightly lit service station with the word 'Glendambo' over the door and a row of tiny cabins. She stopped, filled up, paid and rented a cabin, all easily enough. It occurred to her that she could not drive home again now, even if she wanted to. She tried not to think about how far from anywhere she must be. She was relieved to find a clean bed and bright lights inside the cabin. She was very tired and, for the first time in eleven weeks, Hiam fell asleep straight away.

She was standing over a sink in a spattered, white shirt, up to the shoulders in blood. She felt about frantically in the bubbly mess between her hands and to her relief found the double lobes. It was intact. She lifted it triumphantly, calling for her gloved assistants to steer her to the dining table, upon which her inert patient lay stretched and blue. The knives and forks were arrayed perfectly upon the napkins and she thought to herself: *It is high time I gave the time of day to that nurse.* She positioned herself authoritatively at the head of the table, elbowed the open skull into position and, with extreme gentleness and precision, eased the brain like a soft-boiled egg into the cavity. As it slipped from her hands it rotated unpredictably and came round all wrong in a floating, foetal way. She suddenly discerned twitching limbs and translucent hands, as if seeing it for the first time as the glistening, red curtain fell away from the membrane. It was all wrong, all wrong in every way. She watched as it struggled momentarily and died, thinking dimly that the blue man's day had come. She woke up sweating.

The door opened slowly and a man came in, shrouded in the shadows, too indistinct to be seen as more than a vague silhouette. As he walked up to the bed she could hear him breathing strangely. He sat down on the bed with his back to her. He was crying softly. She suddenly recognised his smell and her fear vanished.

'Masoud!—How did you find me? How did you get here?'

He answered in pure Arabic, not in dialect,

'I flew. I followed your tracks, clear as a fleeing gazelle in the desert. Marks on the gravel, tracks through the foam, and above that, I listened for your voice on the wind, and followed it.'

She reached for him and they embraced, tightly and painfully. She was flooded with a relief which strung her taut with the effort to hold on to it. They lay down, face to face. She stroked his whole body, lightly and harshly, lovingly. When his grief had melted away, they made love, slowly, and then fell asleep in each other's arms.

She woke up, the bed sticky and running with sweat. He was lying with his back to her. She reached out and pulled him towards her from the shoulder. The body rolled unnaturally while the head, left behind, fell forward off the pillow. Her hand was bloody and she screamed. His face was white, eyes closed, the head cleanly severed from his shoulders. The bed was a great pool of cooling blood, seeping over her limbs and crawling all over her body. She screamed in horror and grief.

'Masoud! Don't leave me like this!'

There was a knock on the door.

'Are you OK in there?'

She went cold with fright.

'Yes, yes, I am OK,' she managed to call out, frantically covering the overlarge head and body and the blood with the unstained bits of quilt. 'Quite OK!'

There was silence outside the door and then footsteps fading away. She lifted the quilt. He was gone, taking his blood with him.

She got dressed shakily and stepped outside.

'Glory to God who sleeps not!' she murmured softly.

The world had changed. As far as the eye could see, the earth was red. It wasn't orange, or soil-red, or brown-red, or perhaps it was all of them at once. It was a rich red, glittering deeply in the mid-morning light. She was vaguely aware of having known that somewhere in Australia the land was this colour but the reality of it was startling and stunning. She hadn't realised that by accident she had gone to that very place and she hadn't realised how red it was. It was a stark and impressive place. Looking away from the meagre buildings, a vast, flat land stretched away in profound and richly tapestried monotony. It was red from the edge of the bitumen off into all interstices of the low shrubs and bushes. Even though the land was rich with life and many-coloured bushes, the interstices dominated, and off at the horizon they were all that could be seen. She went into the station and bought a cake for breakfast and went back to the car. She unpacked her gas burner, coffee jar and beaker. Feeling rather happy, distracted, she sat on her suitcase and boiled some water, spooned in three spoons of the rich, brown, aromatic coffee, let it foam up once, twice, three times, and switched off the burner. She felt excited. She was alone but using the camping tools, feeling free. She put her nose over the pot, breathing in the coffee and the faint, lingering cardamom, ground by Masoud. She put the coffee, cake and a cup onto a little tray, put the other things into the boot, shut it and, crossing the road, walked a little way off into the low bushland. She sat on a bare hillock and set down her tray with the still steaming coffee. She stared at the horizon which was becoming more shimmery and unstable as the morning advanced. The sky was already a blue of intense, light purity. Her glance came nearer and nearer, flicking over the frosty, bluish tops of the twisted shrubs, nearer and down to the red sand at her feet. It was faintly rippled. The sun beat on her back and she began to sweat. It really was sand. Sipping, she felt it and ran it between her fingers. It was smooth, still cool sand, metallic pink from one angle, red from every other.

She sat in the growing heat for a while, feeling the sweat run along her body in trickles. It was a pleasant heat, intense and unalloyed. Before long, however, it was too much, and she stood up with her tray and walked back, dispirited. Perhaps this momentary peace, known only once it was leaving her, was all she had left home for. Perhaps this was all that was ever going to be possible and it was time to turn back. She thought of Muhsin and Fatima, her room in their house. She avoided touching mentally her own house.

She phoned them. Muhsin answered.

'Where are you, Hiam?' She felt remote from him, as if in another country.

'Glendambo.'

'Where?'

'It's somewhere north, I think. It must be famous; it's where Australia is red.'

'Oh. Are you all right?'

'As well as can be expected. I think I have to keep going for a while, though. I'm not sure what for.' She began to cry. She hoped he wouldn't ask where she was going.

'You do what you have to do, my sister,' he said gently. 'We are here for you when you need anything.'

'Give my love to Fatima and Amin.' She was sobbing.

'Yes, I will. Go in Peace, my sister.'

She hung up. She was flooded with love for him and Fatima and Amin, and longed for them, but it was certain and stated; she was driving on. *From God we come, and to Him will return.* She muttered the worn-out phrase over and over to herself without thinking, a charm against thought as she pulled out onto the highway.

By midday she was exhausted with driving. The terrible, red and lonely land had taken her up and pushed her on without mercy. She couldn't stop and drove on hating everything she saw. There was blood on the road, on the roadsides, on the battered heads of stiffening black cattle lying on either side. Great black and tawny eagles heaved themselves awkwardly into the air, reluctantly leaving indistinguishable, bloody messes on the shimmering asphalt. The land stretched flat and imprecise to its uniform and evanescent rim. It seemed incredibly small. The sky was an upturned bowl, trapping her like some manic cockroach in a flat nothing. It was intolerable. She had to scrabble on but a feeling of insane irritation intensified with every changeless minute. Sweat poured from her dirty hair down her dirty neck between her sticky breasts and filled her navel, to run off either side around her belly in tickling trickles down between her legs into the sheepskin seatcover. The seat was soaked behind and under her, and stank of sweat and her unkempt, uncared for, stinky self. She was scouring the land in a frantic rage for some sign of something. This could not be remotely necessary or helpful. Every dead cow, disappointed eagle, ragged, half-moon tyre-rubber increased her search and her frustration. This could not be. Most of all it was the land itself that was intolerable. Red forever, seamless, shimmering, unlike anything she had ever imagined. Frosted with blue and green, dotted with unknown and unknowable life, hiding birds she couldn't hear or recognise. What could justify the ongoing pressure on the accelerator? What could she ever say was the point of having seen this or having been here?

A man is a beautiful animal. Hiam looks at Masoud's sleeping body; relaxed limbs, long lashes. Like a gazelle, like a boy from a story: red-gold and black. She remembers a story in which a sleeping boy has his shirt blown up by the wind, exciting a crowd of wondering onlookers to marvel at his beautiful and perfectly formed testicles. She places her hand on the quiet groin, watching his eyes slowly open, waiting for him to reach, reach, reach for her. He is beautiful, very beautiful indeed. The exotic curves, the consistencies of his arm, his chest, delight her. She rolls him over and fingers the domains of his back. His back is a mystery even to him, the dark side of the moon, her private garden, map to her secrets. He can only know of it what she chooses to relay to him.

The land changed. It became uglier, more human, bigger. Huge mounds and burrows, holes and hillocks, old and broken machinery appeared sporadically on either side and then more and more regularly. The earth had lost its redness and took on a washed-out, pinkish colour. She hated it more and enjoyed her hatred more. The intense discomfort left her although the temperature was still rising. The sky lost its rigid, glassy appearance and became molten blue, as vague and imprecise as the land had been before.

Masoud likes Hiam's story of his life. She has told the story many times to Zena, as the preliminary to *her* story.

*There was this man who never saw his home. This man never even saw his home village: it had a place in his mind and heart carved by its absence. He was a man made by the losses his mother had suffered and tempered by her harsh memories. He knew his homeland like a book he had read and reread a thousand times. The story began long long ago. The land was green and dry, lush and stony, ugly and beautiful, of highlands and lowlands, foreground and hinterland. It was the land of the settings of the stories. The Land of Stories. In the stories it was the land of bones and bullets and blood; the land of songs, goats and their young in the highlands, mysterious words, rocks, olives, flowers. In this land of mothers' and grandmothers' voices the air was once heavy with orange blossom and jasmine. In their voices it was once and always the land of the Jann and the dreaming demon. The living dead and the dead living. He loved it but could only look at his memories, not revisit them. The voice of grief and of longing was his earliest memory, since it was the only song his mother ever sang. He was born as a guest in a stranger's house.*

*Death was his father's name and life's work. Death had converted his father into the great well of absence which he and his mother drew from and wept into every day. Far more than his brother, he was his mother's companion, her miracle, for it astounded her that death had not taken the sperm and embryo, the son, into the ground with the father. Her body had swelled while his had rotted away. She named this son Masoud . . .'*

She has seen him before, listening at the door, and later he looks sideways into her eyes, warm and wordless. Zena, for her part, loves how sad the story is before she came along. It makes her feel powerful.

She found herself in an ugly town which boasted of its underground hotels and museums and graves. She sat sideways in the car with the door open, parked in the shade of a billboard which showed a giant, faded opal, rather like a mouldy pizza. Across the dusty road three thin, yellowish dogs lay sleeping under a Car of Islam. Up the road a Greyhound tour bus streaked with red sand stood oddly on three wheels and a car jack. There was no-one in sight. The land and the town and the sky seemed to have lost their distinctness from each other, to have decomposed into one another.

The Car of Islam suddenly roared off. She jumped. She had seen no-one. She winced and without thought looked for the dogs. All three were standing, unharmed, dishevelled and sleepy, where the car had been. One was much younger than the other two and was eyeing them with a deferential if implicitly swaggering air. It was by far the healthiest looking, gold and almost glossy, like a wheatfield. The largest was a scrawny male who twitched at irregular intervals just enough to interfere with the rhythm of his movements. He was scarred and dirty with a pelt like an unkempt, weedy paddock but nonetheless not pitiable. He looked tough, mad and ugly. He began to walk jerkily, aiming himself in the general direction of the bus. The other two looked up the road, then stared straight at Hiam, or rather at her occupation of the billboard shade, and then sauntered after him. They caught up with him quite quickly and, without apparent reason, all three stopped simultaneously in the middle of the road. They all froze. The tough one suddenly snarled into the silent air, without even looking at them, and continued towards the bus. The other adult waited a moment, turned and stalked off in the opposite direction, across the road and disappeared down an alley between two nondescript shops. The young dog crumpled in indecision, looking either way up and down, golden on the faded, grey road. She felt a rush of affection for it. Like many things, it too seemed somehow familiar. Finally it wandered aimlessly but predictably towards the bus and sat down in the sun, settling in for a long stare at the expanse of shade underneath. She had lost the chance to notice the third dog. It was neither young and beautiful, nor odd and grand.

The land intensified to a deep red as soon as she left the town. She drove in stretches through the day, stopping until she couldn't bear stopping, and driving until she couldn't bear driving. She could get no peace.

Hiam loves Zena to be praised and worried over. She even shows her daughter off, in hints and guesses, to strangers. To Australians.

On the train with Zena, Hiam has no fear. Zena is her charm and her link with Australians. They too have daughters and they too love them and are proud of them. She looks around at the people, imagining them imagining: What a beautiful daughter that woman has! Alone in the train, without Zena, she thinks of them looking at her and thinking: Foreigner.

Zena sits next to her, conversing loudly enough to be heard, which also pleases Hiam. On the train (and only on the train), she loves the fact that Zena speaks English like an Australian.

'How long will I be going to school?'

'A long time, and when you finish school you will go to university like your mum and dad.'

(What an intelligent family that beautiful intelligent little girl comes from!)

'Kindergarten–school–university. That's long, isn't it Mum?'

'Yes, and after, you will have a job, a profession. What would you like to do?'

'Ride a bicycle.'

'As a job? No, you will go to university, and be a doctor or something, and then get married, with a beautiful, white dress, the most beautiful in the world. You will be a princess!'

Zena looks very thoughtful. 'That must be after the bicycle.'

'Yes.'

'And after?'

'After what?'

'The dress.'

'Then you will live happily ever after.'

'For how long?'

'Years and years and years.'

'I could ride the bicycle then.'

'Mmmm.'

'I would have to take the dress off to ride the bicycle.'

When Zena has her mind set on something, she simply veers and swerves to avoid Hiam's improvisations. Hiam has begun to feel that she has to learn a new language.

The sunset was shocking. She stopped the car a little off the road and leaned against it, staring westward, thinking vague half thoughts as the sky melted smoothly from its flushed fire to a fading, cooling red glory. She felt a slight vertigo and could almost hear the pulsing rush of great wings beating. She felt as if she was flying through it rather than looking on. Yes, she was moving very fast on the inside whenever she stopped still. She entered a kind of stasis only when she drove.

She dreamed she was on the shore of some Australian town, Adelaide-ish but small, looking for a place to swim. One part of the beach was said to have too many sharks but she went to check anyway. It had big and little sharks, blue, black, and bloody ones. Some large ones were threshing the water, making it foam in a small circle. She saw the black fins in the froth now and then, like jagged rocks. Smaller sharks were cruising near the shore and quite tiny ones regarded her with a speculative air from the shallows. She thought of swimming by the jetty, and asked someone. 'Oh yes, its quite safe there.' She went to the jetty. The water was murky, even dirty, with lumps of clothes drifting by, all in one direction. She looked, and saw that they were dead, derelict men, their rags parting over their swollen, bluish bellies. A naked woman, navel up, drifted by, her face clouded by skeins of hair. Then a child, a little round belly and frail ribs. A slow cavalcade of bodies, shaken in an unnaturally lively way now and then by unseen little sharks. She couldn't swim, and sat down dispiritedly with sweat filling her shoes.

Dreams pushed her to drive on even at night.

She had only stopped to eat, to defecate, urinate, sleep. When she slept she dreamed of the road. Time and time again (but perhaps it was only once) she had stopped and sat in the car, thinking blankly for hours the same non-thoughts. Only fragments of meaning could break through the humming after-shocks of the road and the inescapable timelessness of every experience. Everything she did seemed to have been done a thousand times and to never end. The road was inside and outside, the waking, sleeping, soothing, tearing nightmare. Sooner or later she would get up and drive again.

She killed. Her undesired and uneaten prey, rabbits by night and birds by day, fell side to side and died where they lay. She killed with the collusion of the car and the road but remained a spectator. Kangaroos, eagles, black cows, calves and bulls all lay rotting on either side in the hazy heat of the day. The ways of the road, its choices and the destinies woven with it, were unknown and unfathomable. The road gave the future ceaselessly; and took everything in one moment without cause or warning. She passed several dead cars, as well. One car had died and rusted halfway up a tree. The only tree for centuries. She passed a freshly killed car—smashed and bloody.

A kangaroo had killed it. Kangaroos were enormous, dead and alive, and some of them were red like the soil. It was clear that if she hit a kangaroo, it would die. But this was no simple hierarchical universe—a simple system for the random killing of animals. The road could take her life too, at any moment, by kangaroo. For a while she had thought that this seemed fair. After a time, however, the bodies of kangaroos—matted, bloody, bloated, broken, seeping, decayed, picked by suicidal foxes, dogs, birds and the wind and the sand—beat like a drum in her chest. The accumulation of images of all the stages of damaged and decaying flesh, skin and bone eroded any certainties and rubbed her raw. Kangaroos were telling her something with a cipher of broken bodies. She hoped fervently that *she* wouldn't hit one and stopped driving much from nightfall to midnight: the Kangaroo Hours. She dreamed of driving instead. In her dreams she slithered whimpering over the broken bodies, unable to stop, wheels sliding with no grip in the blood. She waited for a smash to black out the bloody road and the horror of driving on and on over the carcases of the dead.

Sooner or later she would get up and drive again. Until the early dawn it was soft little thuds of little bodies, little knocks, instant deaths tossed blindly to this side and that. These were the Rabbit Hours: slow or fast they died, brained by the bumper, axle, or mashed by the wheels. She couldn't stand it and, sooner or later, she stopped again and tried to sleep on the back seat. The road of dreams was more explicitly macabre but less memorable and not her responsibility.

At the end of a predawn, as the world slumped back into an empty darkness as if reluctant to face the day, the animals stiffened into bushes and shrubs and other harmless grotesqueries making meaningless gesticulations in any direction. The world seemed to become lighter but to lose vigour and colour. The rich moonlit silhouettes of trees and bushes and the gently undulating horizon had disappeared. Everything except the sky had become one soft continuous grey blanket peppered with dull black figures and shapes which were largely unidentifiable. The only sound she could hear was the powerful drone of the engine but it was so unremarkably blended with her bodily sensations that she felt profoundly deaf to the world. She no longer sounded the horn or saw kangaroos.

Her thoughts were as indistinguishable as the greying land. A thick blanket enveloped her, seemed to emanate from her. The road, the land and her self had become one and the same thing. Even her most painful thoughts seemed more like the carcases of dead animals she knew were strewn across the road-way—almost unremarkable, almost expected, almost unnoticed.

With the dawn the first thing which took on any colour was blood on the road. She saw the road divided and pitted by a jagged crevasse of too-rich, liquid black. She turned to the east where the sun was about to rise. A few pale, golden rays seemed to be struggling, even failing in their attempt to pierce some watercolour clouds clumped above the horizon. The sun rose and seemed to hang cold, intensely white and static above the murky world. She looked back to the road and felt as if she and the car were also painted. Idle, still, never moving, never changing. She was the viewer painted into a picture which therefore never needed to be seen by anybody else. The road ahead cleaved the dimly lit land in unmoving, geometric lines. The flicker of a shadow of a passing bush was ethereal and feeble in comparison with the unshakeable fixity of the scene. Fixed unmoving in the passenger window shone another light in the west. It caught her eye and she turned her gaze westwards. The luminous disc of the massive moon was crisper than the eastern light, but gave even less light, if any at all. She faced north and focused on the fading glimmer of last night's stars. Something unwelcome inside her shook her as she felt herself driving on a still landscape with each profile lit and shadowed, driving between the sun and the moon.

*Does the road continue to eternity?*

It was, in the end, the most beautiful dawn she could remember. Blue, coniferous-looking bushes had halos of the purest gold, and the thousand-times wrung and twisted trunks of the occasional, scrubby trees were highlighted, showing a peculiar grace in their wiry forms which she was sure they had not possessed before. Their muscular arms were reflective, as glossy as burnished copper or healthy horses. Shining like nothing she had seen before. Their foliage shone like an animal's coat, waving gaily above the red earth. The heat of the coming day showed promise to flatten everything but even its menace was at dawn a harsh joy.

Day driving was a relief. It was sticky, unbearably hot, clean and neat. It was exactly what it seemed to be. The dead lay on the verges, simply dead. Except for the occasional bird, the living stayed away. The animals believed in her during the day: they knew she was dangerous and stayed out of the way. Only at night did they believe she was illusory and stand and stare, and die in wonder.

She had never understood Australia. She had never understood Australians. She had never known that there was so much outside of herself and her world. It was frightening to know that this road had waited through the years of her incomprehension. It had been here the whole time.

A young man on a battered motorbike, with long, rope-like hair streaming like broom brush from his bare head appears at the side of the bus as Hiam looks out of the window. She feels Zena's sweaty body lean against her to look. He rides alongside for a while, his head thrust forward, with a reddish beard quivering and parting in the breeze on his chin. He bounces slightly too much with the bumps in the road, every line of his body expressing joy in the hot, summer air. The noise of his machine buzzes and rumbles intolerably in the sticky bus and his exhaust wafts in through the open windows. Just then he looks up at the hot faces of the row of passengers. He has piercing, silly blue eyes, and a slow smile of delight spreads over his face, as if he is treasuring something. Suddenly he stands up full length on the bike pedals, brings his grinning face close to an open window and screams into the expectant air,

'You're all VIRGINS!!' in a voice that seems to be itching with uncontrollable happiness.

He zooms off in cheeky, self-confident immunity and is gone. The noise of the bus engine intensifies, showing the driver's irritation, and the passengers mutter and shuffle, exchanging indiscernible mumbles and whispers of disgust. Strangers turn to each other and shake their heads. Hiam sits and reddens in perplexity. None of the people around her understand. She wonders for the millionth time how she can ever understand this place. It is incomprehensible to its own. She suddenly becomes aware of Zena's breathing next to her. The girl is sneakily, secretly laughing. She swings round to her and looks into her eyes. They are lit up and very happy. Irrepressible. She stares. Has Zena understood? Is she merely enjoying everyone's discomfort or giggling at the word 'virgins'? But Zena suddenly leans over her and looks up the road to see if she can still see the cyclist. *She understands this language which means nothing.* Hiam leans to Zena and whispers into her ear without thinking,

'What did he mean?'

Zena looks into her confused eyes and laughs.

'Nothing. He was just happy. It's like graffiti.'

Hiam feels quite happy, suddenly, and smiles into Zena's face. She thinks about the boy on the bike. She remembers that she did notice his happiness. She knew that it meant nothing, too. She really understood the parts and was not so far away from the whole. She looks at Zena with respect. They both gaze out of the window, enjoying the graffiti shimmering in the heat on the streetside walls.

She thought suddenly: the road may well be the truth revealed but there are no onlookers here. No-one will ever know Hiam in a Jumpsuit in a Red Landscape. She smiled.

'Have you really shown or talked about everything in your life to someone?'

She couldn't remember.

She was momentarily cheered, even reassured. Then Hiam the Australian Tour Guide began to parade through her mind.

'You wouldn't believe how red!'

The ladies hung on her words. Maybe they would all make a trip of it. The Ladies at Ayers Rock. In hats.

Zena has a skill as a professional taster. She is very popular at the parties because she knows almost infallibly who cooked the kibbi, the felafel, the *waraq al-'ainab* by a single mouthful.

'The hand of Auntie Maryam,' she pronounces, and, pausing amid the general laughter,

'And Caroline stirred!'

This is a joke of long standing between Zena and Hiam. In private, Zena tells her that all have signatory sins of omission or commission. In one story, a mother faints away upon tasting a dish, recognising the hand of her twenty-years-lost son, Badr ad-Din Hassan, the son of the Wazir of Basra. Zena says, 'I should think so too.'

She passed through a town very similar to one she had passed through hours before. Her life had been a test run. Wound up, pushed into circumstances to see how it was done or where her stress points were. Bad on rough terrain—no brakes. She was the demonstration model: Hiam the student, Hiam the bride, Hiam the wife. Hiam the cook, the hostess, the committee member. Hiam the mother, the teacher, the home economist.

The story teller, the schemer.

The Widow.

Hiam is watching Masoud watching Zena. Zena is at the table doing her homework, biting her lower lip upon which Hiam can make out the traces of hastily scrubbed away lipstick. Zena's black hair is coiled to the side, falling into shadow off her shoulder. It is so massed that it looks like a black cat asleep on her shoulders, embracing her. Masoud is also biting his lip. He looks uncertain and apprehensive. He is holding his breath, as if he believes that holding his breath will hold her still in the chair.

He leans forward suddenly, his eyes bright. He murmurs in her ear,

'Study hard and you might become an engineer like your father!'

'*Da'ad!*'

Zena turns on him, spinning the cat off her shoulder in disarray.

'You are a taxi driver, *not* an engineer!'

Hiam leaps forward. The small triangle of still-life love has become a flurry of arms and voices.

'Zena! Your father is a very educated man! He finished his degree in Amman. He has the highest qualifications. Apologise at once!'

Zena stares her down for a moment, fierce and powerful. Hiam realises that this was aimed at her.

'Yeah, yeah, yeah. Sorry Dad.'

Hiam watches Masoud's face. It is empty of expression, a look which makes him resemble Zena when she is asleep.

Zena watches Hiam watching Masoud and then rips her books off the table and disappears down the corridor, shaking the house.

She ran through images with both bitterness and pleasure. It was a nice distraction to define everything. She was on the endless road, stretching to infinity ahead and behind. She had always been on it. Now it was visible, its grinding rhythm underneath her audible. If this is a test run, when does my life begin? She was enjoying herself, in a twisted way. If one could think and think, using only the abstract, or symbols, then . . . Before and After are places, knots on a string, roadside shrubs. Now is infinites-imally different in its grasses, rocks, bones and dust from, say—*Now*.

She thought of the kangaroos. She had turned the hidden fabric of life into a visible world. A red land, an interminable road, populated by beasts with whom she spoke not, but killed without intention or retribution. She was both the wrath of God and a meaningless illusion, hurtling through their world. The kangaroos lived, got scared, grazed, played, and died.

'Why are all beasts more blessed than I?'

Hiam is peeling an enormous garlic bulb which proves to be a single clove. She cuts the fat clove in two. A garlic bulb in Spring, swelling and bursting with its thickened shaft forming and then pushing through its centre, searching for the surface of the absent soil. She sees it clearly, revealed in the two halves, and she thinks of the swelling penis and the swelling belly as the same moment, the same miracle, the same slow excitement beyond chance or inten-tion. *Masoud, Hiam, Zena, searching for the garden soil.*

She was crying so violently with rage that she couldn't see the road. She pulled off the highway erratically and leapt out of the car. She ran in a frantic, superhuman frenzy into the scrub, stumbling and scuffling over the hillocks, screams welling up in her. She was so angry that she felt as though she was flying. She began to scream aloud, screaming abuse at Masoud and had to stop running in order to blast him. She leapt and spun and kicked sand into the air like a creature in a strange courtship dance, indiscriminately ripping at the bushes and tossing them furiously away from her.

*'Yal'an abuka! Yakhrib baytak!* Why did you give up? Years, years, years ago, you gave up on me! You deserted me! Shame on you, unfaithful man! You son of shit! How could you leave me? Years ago, years, years, years, in the little world of the taxi, car full of self-pity! How could you?'

She raced through the same thoughts, the same words, over and over again, more and more quietly. She slowly stopped spinning and hurling foliage at nothing. She sat down, punching the ground vaguely, softly, murmuring,

'Masoud, Masoud, why did you not stick to me. Why did you turn hurt and weak and quiet. God damn you—damn you. Masoud, why did you desert Hiam, whom you loved, and who loved you.'

She fell silent, stroking the smooth sand, running it in fake rills and falls down the slope away from her. She watched it flow between her fingers and the thought came up: Hiam, why did you leave Masoud in a strange land and escape yourself with your daughter?

She thought to herself that there was something monstrous and unique about a life; hers, Masoud's, Zena's. Hers had been turned inside out. Once eviscerated, there was no pattern by which to reconstitute it. Each life was a barely understood new species, some kind of hybrid monster. Hers was displayed before her in parts but there was no manual and no sense to them. It had scattered into unconnected shards which seemed never to have been part of the same thing. No recognisable liver, heart, or alimentary system could be clearly defined, waiting there to be put back into its place in a coherent scheme. There was no clear way to tell her story straight.

The scattered dots, lines, metallic strip, the rising suns, the scattered and shuddering stars spinning and twirling ahead and behind made her suddenly feel as though she was being unravelled. The road was her thread. She had pulled out onto the highway, unravelling, unravelling that dreamy life; birth, girlhood, study, marriage, Zena, Masoud. Ahead, her life was a shocking cipher; a blank, a hollowness in the stomach, a hollowness under the bitumen, a hollowness behind the eyes, a profound incoherence in all words and structures. The sunlight and the clouds, the bushes and the dead corpses whisking by had a very thin fabric, a veneer over the emptiness of reality. Her hand on the steering wheel was as hollow as an unused rubber glove. She began to cry in fear. Why had Masoud cast her into this terrible nothingness?

The spasm passed. She thought dully: I was seen by you, therefore I was. One is made by being perceived. She imagined Masoud's eyes on her, as they had always been. She was filled with yearning for his glance and to be who she had been under it. She drifted away. Masoud was next to her. She refashioned him slowly, lovingly, the limbs at ease, the hawk in the eyes, the beautiful lips, Zena's lips. She then warmed up the glance and turned the head her way. She rested his glance on her shoulder, her ear, the glossy, long black hair, lovingly down the elegant neck. She practised a flippant, sideways glance of her own to meet his, laughter in her eyes, luminous, seductive, black-fringed eyes. She acted herself; the typical smile, concern, shock, the pleasant surprise, comradely teasing, amusement, a slight laugh, desire. She parted her lips, glancing sideways, lovingly, laughingly, at him, radiant, confident, impressive at the wheel. How he loved her! For a while she was totally engrossed. The car hurtled along the whipping ribbon at 180 km. A truck's form filled her vision and then its airstream crumpled and rocked the buzzing peace in the cabin for a split second. She suddenly imagined the little bubble from the outside, from outside the splattered windscreen. A mad, dishevelled woman, posing and talking, miming another woman to nobody, alone in a car. She slowed down, dizzy and nauseous. She decided to stop driving for the day and began searching for a place to rest.

The road had become so monotonous that it seemed stale and familiar. She slowed and rolled to a halt in the next roadside stop. Her body was singing and her head dizzy from the driving. She walked unsteadily to stare at the road, the late sun full on her chest.

It was really just a road. A very long road. It was mysterious only because she hadn't bothered to find out where it went, which showed only that she was crazy. She was travelling with all the purpose of a pilgrimage for no reason and with no knowledge. For all she knew it could end suddenly in the trackless desert, meandering off first into a maddened trail and then into incoherent kangaroo prints. It might, but she couldn't imagine it. She walked to the edge and put her palms on the bitumen. It was too hot to touch but solid and rough. She peered south with her face near the ground, then north. They both seemed too real, and wrong. It was very real and ordinary, just endless. She felt a bit panicked. How could she ever tell someone about it not being just a road when it so obviously was? Her life had become a horrible, incoherent, unmapped secret which she had to carry alone.

She suddenly looked at the setting sun with a

rush of horror. Her scalp crawled and the wings beat loudly.

It was setting in the east.

She curled up in the back seat of the car with the quilt, too discouraged to eat and too depressed to worry about safety. The journey might have no purpose that she could articulate, but to have driven the wrong way for most of the day was a crushing disaster.

Going was better than stopping; and there was a right and a wrong direction.

The cold came on as if something was lifted from the senses in one swift movement. Her bones and muscles stiffened and began to ache and she was driven out into the chill, young moonlight to pin the little tent into a hollow in the sand.

She awoke with a shudder. It was still desert-cold but the tent was not in darkness. She could see the tumbled quilt in all its folds, the book, with its gilded letters glowing faintly, her bag, her clothes. There was a faint, even pure light outside. Wrapped in the quilt, she crawled out and sat at the tent opening. She could see clearly the muted colours of the pale blue, pale green, smoky shrubs, the muted colour of the red earth, dark as blood. The sky was glowing, the piercing, painful brilliance of the stars faded to a few intense, white diamonds. She heard a distant groan, distant as a broken chant, and she saw a herd of camels, wild, unkempt camels shimmering pale blue and silver, glistening with drops of water. The mothers called their calves, warmly, warningly, nigglingly. Amongst the legs, the calves loped at ease. Stretched out, the line looked like the tasselled fringe of the curtain of the sky. They filed past her a little distance away, under the fading stars. She watched until they were gone, crept back into the tent and slept deeply until the heat of the morning sun beat her awake.

She was again in the red Australian desert, with a long line of bull ants methodically removing her food and disappearing beyond view off into nowhere.

Saturday morning and Zena is at Jennifer's. Hiam and Masoud lie in bed, listening to the silence. Without warning, they make love. They have breakfast and, as Masoud is leaving, he takes her face in his hands and kisses her. He rests the side of his face against hers and looks deeply into her eye, too close for focus. His eye fills her vision as a dark, vague pool, frank and shocking. She looks in and takes in part of what he means. He says nothing and walks out the door without looking back. Hiam stands for a moment and then goes into the kitchen. She is assailed by something unclear, a foggy vertigo. She stands by the table, trembling, and then reaches out her hand and smashes the plate and cup he used.

The cicadas buzzed and screamed in her ears, reso-
nating painfully in her skull. More than anything else
their humming, sizzling mating call made her feel
mad. She did not dare to ask about the sound, in case
she was the only person on earth who was hearing
it. She overheard a wild-eyed boy mutter that it was
driving him crazy but even then she suspected a
trick. Who was the wild-eyed boy? She started seeing
tamarinds and camels everywhere. Were they really
tamarinds? Really camels?

Although the road led to towns and villages, big and
small, this had lost all significance. The last name she
could remember clearly was Glendambo but there
had been many since then. The road inevitably led
out of them as well, as if they had never been. They
meant nothing.

Every day had become one day, and each day was
fragmented and scattered in the prismatic mad
mirror of everyday. Her mind ran over the moments
until they made up an inchoate whole. They ran into
each other like accumulating water droplets and she
could no longer imagine having not driven the highway. How many times had she stopped and how
many times had she thought again over the events
and motivations of stopping? How many times had

she pulled off the road, set up her little tent in the twilight, in the night, and slept in the eye of the nightmare storm, pinned in a cocoon to the unstable earth? Pinned like a beetle displayed to the sky? How many unrestful nights had been followed by panic-struck mornings, panicked to keep moving, followed by days on the road? How many times had she accidentally driven the wrong way? She could not be sure. It might have been once but it had also been as long as she could remember. One night was different, illuminated, but she could not remember which one. It seemed long ago. Coherence and sequence had been wiped out by the hum, the repetition of the scratched record, the highway, and the manic need to keep the machine running.

She ran and reran each moment in her mind, searching for a meaning, or something meaningful, or a theory of meaning. Slowly the edges between what had really happened and what she had thought thereafter dissolved. It occurred to her that she might really be somewhere else altogether but it couldn't be somewhere nice. On the other hand, her eighteen years in Australia seemed to have been leading inevitably and inexorably, ruthlessly to this inescapable *Now*. How would Hiam, dishevelled and unwashed, deal with this one? 'A fine intelligence. Will go far.'

Hiam tells herself that she will write poetry but she writes, or thinks of writing, very rarely. She tells stories to Zena; and with beautiful, unscarred, perfect Zena, she enters an ideal world, a timeless world in which she and Zena, and the spirit of her absent mother shut out Masoud's unhappiness and ignore his existence. Hiam tells Zena a story and goes to bed healed and simplified. Zena knows that the stories help her mother sleep and she also loves them.

'Mum, Mum, quick—tell me a story to make it better!'

Masoud can find no consolation.

*His beautiful and spirited daughter, wild as a flower, or a gazelle, startled and brave, brings him no consolation.* Hiam is angry and keeps Zena to herself, stopping herself from telling him about her movements, comments and jokes. He is exiled from his own joy in her and he is afraid of what she thinks of him.

What could it signify? The road was the protagonist's straitjacket, the car her prison, or her skull; her self on the thread of life. Too clumsy. She was only now her own random ideas and experiences. She laughed. Academic theories of long roads. She felt suddenly cheerful and accelerated into a daydream of road meanings. Begin with a dictionary definition and then say something surprising and clever. A road: a constructed means of getting from one place to another. Symbolically, life and the path through it. In her case, the protagonist is seen to be experiencing a purgatory of repetition, or a hell of eternal suffering. Perhaps heaven. How could the road be heaven? The path of non-being and dissolution? Fail: the road is not heaven, and yet this was to her the most persuasive. The stilted ideas trotted by like low trees and stunted bushes, and the road accommodated them. She felt mentally dry and rusty. Hiam with the University Education was strangely inadequate out in the red, while the road's readiness to be anything from her lover to the unravelling skein of human psyche was disturbing. The road was obliging every time and she left the game in disgust.

Hiam is feeling very alone in the empty house. She lies on the bed, staring upward at the white ceiling, tracing and retracing the tortured path of a hairline crack in the plaster. Her arms are spread wide like the gliding wings of a bird of prey and, motionless, she follows the trail as if it is the earth almost indecipherable beneath her. She isn't thinking about it with any attention but she feels it through a vague, plunging vertigo. She feels this, however, whenever she really thinks about Masoud. She lies back, thinking, bored. The house is clean, the garden uncompelling, three hours until Zena gets home from school. Locked in on the trail. Masoud is driving. Masoud is always driving. The spangled light in the bedroom picks out all the minute, frenetic particles suspended with her in the air. She suddenly notices the cracked ceiling and closes her eyes. The vertigo stops and the phone rings.

Jennifer wants Zena to stay over.

'She has too much homework,' Hiam says quickly, realising as she says it that Jennifer knows better than she what homework Zena has. Hiam almost panics at the thought that she might have to spend the evening alone. If only Masoud would get sick and have to stay home for a while.

Jennifer doesn't argue but she tells Zena that her mum is upset.

She shuts her eyes against the ceiling cracks so long that she falls asleep on top of the bedclothes.

Daily she awoke and as she rose she descended. Consciousness pulled her down into something worse than dreams, into the maelstrom, accompanied by a poison wind which blasted the audible scream from her brain. She knew she had lost her sanity. This didn't surprise her, in fact it seemed reasonable under the circumstances.

'*Habibti, No-one* could stay sane under those circumstances!'

What surprised her was how physical madness was—this she had never imagined. This shaking, sweating, reeling, heart-thumping, scalp-crawling; as if she was arrested in the once-in-a-lifetime moment in front of a firing squad, with conclusion forever *Now*, and forever deferred. Sick to the point of vomiting she floated down a street, muttering to herself '*Now. Now. Now.*' It seemed like a thousand times that she followed Masoud or Zena, or saw them, or heard them. The people around her would not stop speaking about them. The panic rose and was held in a plateau phase. She could almost sense the truth that all of them were stating between their lines or whispering behind their palms to her. Under no circumstances could a single face, one man in hundreds of millions, ever again be Masoud. Everyone became him, pushing her towards and then withholding the fact that not one was real. She played with and panicked about the many Masouds in the crowd.

One of them stole her handbag. After the brief shock of losing all her ID, and after finding her credit card in her pocket, she didn't care. But she mentally named the town *Ain al-Liss*, Thief Springs.

Masoud how could you leave me? Masoud, Masoud, our Zena has killed herself.

Their lovemaking takes on an aspect of the giving and taking of reassurance. Hiam makes love, loving him and weeping for him, trying to make him know that he is loved. None of it is a lie but it changes their lovemaking. She loses the self-engrossed abandon and pleasure which so delighted him and which would have reassured him more than her earnest passion and desperation. Hiam is a wise lover but she doesn't know how to return to careless love. They no longer talk frankly because of his admiration and mistrust of her, so too much is left unsaid which has to be wordlessly told in the sex. Too much is being carried by the sex. It is no longer the joy of expressing themselves in just another variation on the theme of love but has become the sole expression of togetherness that recalls their past. It is the proof of all and sex cannot survive that. For Hiam this is grief upon grief and she is afraid that Masoud will misinterpret the change.

Gradually she begins to look, rather than touch. She loves him but making love to him is too hard. Each time she makes love to him she has to travel. She collects herself together and marches the long stretch to be intimate beside him. Each time she has to make herself rediscover looking into him rather than looking at him. It takes effort and he never takes a step towards her. He always waits. It isn't that he doesn't want to make love. He does. It is as if he has no comprehension of the effort it takes to enter the prerequisite intimacy. She journeys dutifully towards him often but sometimes it is easier to stay away, strong and inviolate.

She loses herself in Zena and watches Masoud lose himself in nothingness, from the outside.

Her body ached for Masoud. How would he take away now the sensual strike in her belly? She thought of his smell, like salt of the sea, his breathing, his eyes holding hers, living in moments the threshold of possible fulfilment. The rhythm and the entangled effort of the human trying to be like water. The terrible, the stupid and the wonderful feeling of love, love, love, love, love, love, love, love, love, love. Where was the noise and the unguarded abandon, the shouting and the rolling, the making love when they were young?

The cicadas sang dryly and incessantly in her ears. The noises in her head had taken a mad, external form. The world outside seemed to be sucking its identity out of her head the further north she crept. The fact that the station attendant had told her they were cicadas didn't give them complete reality, since she wasn't sure that she hadn't also invented the attendant. She wondered if they stopped singing while she was asleep.

Masoud had died in stages because she had stopped seeing him. She had retracted the life-giving glance, and he had wilted, stiffened, dried and died, desiccated by her neglect. It was too late too late too late. In the end he had not even had the strength to take her with him.

Hiam begins to tell stories to delay Zena from going out. She spends all of her time weaving the imperceptible skein to hamper Zena's movements, slowing every move down without the girl's knowledge. She begins to lie to her daughter, hates doing it, but still does. Zena also begins to lie. Lies become their currency; they exchange and trade, negotiate and deal. A lie can purchase life and freedom and Zena gets into high finance. She feels no qualms. Her loyalty to her parents, and her loyalty to herself and her friends are all absolute. She cushions and protects her parents with her lies and lives free and generously for her friends. Her parents' commands and bribes cannot detain her for she senses that they are as loving and dishonest with her as she is with them. Hiam knows and it drives her crazy.

'I have become the parrot telling stories to prevent the infidelities of a young wife.'

She grounds Zena on any flimsy pretext. She trades: two more hours television with girlfriends for a Saturday night. Home by 10 pm; but if you go with your cousin Amin, 12 midnight.

More and more she blames Australia, the land of damage and imprisonment. Australia forces the mother to become the hunter, setting the snares. Australia. The word which transforms the living into heartless stone.

She sat on a bench in a mall, listening to the laments of the women:

'My daughter ran away with a boy.'

'My husband ran away with a woman.'

'It might have been my son your daughter ran away with.'

'It might have been my daughter.'

'It might have been mine.'

'Or mine.'

' . . . my daughter . . . ' ' . . . dead . . . ' ' . . . my husband . . . ' ' . . . died . . . ' ' . . . it's hard . . . '
' . . . is dead . . . '

'He' 'She' 'I'

'*Mum*! How come Khalti Jamila thinks I am getting married to Amin? What did you say to her?'

'Hiam, by the eyes of my three children, I told her nothing!'

Jamila swears everything by the eyes of her three children, who all wear glasses.

Auntie Jamila is on the phone to the Defence Advocate of the Police Complaints Tribunal. Everyone gathers around and listens.

'No Dear, the detective *punched* my son. It is Unnecessary Force, Police Brutality, and we have laid the Complaint.'

That's telling them! Everyone waits.

'No, Officer. I do not want the apology!'

'No, Dear. I do not want compensation!'

She shakes her ornate, auburn coiffure as the advocate speaks.

'No, Dear. I do not want court cases!'

She inhales.

'What do I want?' In the voice of the smoothest reason, '*All* I want, Dear, is the Hand that struck my son brought to me on a Silver Platter.'

She pauses, then,

'And not the Other One!'

Akram has just been accepted into Law School.

'We will all go and watch Akram in the court,' Imm Akram says delightedly. 'He will have a wig. Yes—we will make a ladies' day out, hats, and a luncheon!'

It is a dream of simple delight which some share and of which some are envious. Auntie Fatima smiles bitterly. Amin has just appeared in the court in a very public case, charged with cultivation. He asserted that the plants were for personal use as eloquently (and with as much success) as his mother argued to the ladies that they were only for selling to Australians.

'Yes, Widad is working,' Uncle Samir says uncomfortably. 'In a good, decent bank. She is a good girl and loves her parents. And of course when she marries—next year, God willing—she will stop working.'

'What makes you so sure?' Zena asks abruptly, with a little annoyance.

'We will tell her to,' he says, simply.

Widad smiles secretively at Zena. *As if.*

Independence has become a dirty word. Anyone who has ever been independent now has to defend and excuse themselves.

'I left home at age twelve because I had to work in Beirut—my family were so poor,' hiding *I left because my mother was dead, my father unhappy, my stepmother cruel, and I ran away, crying my child's heart out of my body forever.*

'My daughter-in-law Su'ad is a good girl, from a good family. But why is she studying still? Why does she want a PhD? She has already caught a good man.'

A wave of sadness sweeps over Hiam. What has happened to her people? They are lost in the desert and are passing the time with the game of who marries whom. Despite his pomposity she knows that Uncle Yusuf is an intelligent, if simple, man so she says what will soothe him,

'The educated woman will give much to her children.'

'She is studying Women's Literature,' he says sadly. It is incomprehensible and might ruin the marriage.

Hiam remembers studying the poet Al-Khansa', the wild cow, who buried her sons and her husbands in war, but never lost her proud voice. She feels too sad to argue. Her own education makes her suspect in this little world where parents struggle to manoeuvre their children into the unthreatening marriage and then believe themselves to be the marriage bond. Her friends and relatives are living in the beds of their children. She looks at Zena. Zena, wild and free, with her purity, loveliness and faith. Zena will choose her own love as has her mother before her. Hiam is open-minded.

'Regardless of religion or nationality, ya Fatima, believe me, *any* Arab who loves Zena and is loved by her.'

'Farida has fallen in love on the computer!' Farida has fallen in love with Sami and chats with him every day on the internet. Technology takes on a new dimension for the Aunties and formerly implacable fathers suddenly cave in on the longstanding request for internet in the home. Farida and Sami have never met but, without any help from their parents and relatives, they have found each other from the opposite ends of the earth. He is doing a PhD, or has finished a PhD, or something adequately impressive in UCLA, California. She is embarking on a PhD in Melbourne. His family is from Ras al-Jabal in Lebanon, hers from Bayt Jaras, 20 km away. They haven't yet seen each other, but she has told her parents, he has told his sister, and inexorable and rapid wheels are in motion.

Her father rings her grandfather and asks about the bridegroom-to-be's family.

*Jiddu* is non-committal. He knows them. Decent people. But he is disturbed, ruffled.

'*Ya waladi*, there are many fine young men of good family here in Ras al-Jabal. Why does she have to go all the way to Bayt Jaras for a husband?'

Her memories ranged themselves before her, inert. She could select, as if selecting a CD. Play this one. Not that one. She tried to play mainly memories of Zena or of other people. Sometimes idly, for no reason except delay. Sometimes because it was good to tell the pain as if it were someone else's. But many clamoured to be played.

Zena. Zena screams,

'You are so stupid! Why won't you even try to enjoy life here? I can see through you. You are an invalid in this house to try to turn me into a nurse. You are in love with worry and pain and if you didn't have this you would invent something!'

Hiam watches the latticed window reflected on the iris of Zena's eye, a technique she has developed to avoid her own feelings. It is erased by a blink and then, shimmering, reforms. Something suddenly flies onto the graph of the eye window and she looks at Zena around the eye and sees wonder in the smooth eyes and face. She turns around. A wet hawk, scared and staring, a *bazi*, is flapping and spattering against the pane. It freezes for a moment, wings outstretched under the overflowing gutter, its beak half open in an inaudible scream. It looks in with one hooded, luminous eye and then it falls off the sill and out of sight, reappearing flying away in the rain.

'What was that?' Zena says, all anger erased in the instant.

'A *bazi*.'

'What is a *bazi*?'

'A *bazi* is—' she thinks about it—spiralling in the sun, spiralling in the evening stories her Yemeniya aunt had told. She doesn't want to give a pebble for a *bazi*. 'It's another word for a *saqer*.'

'What is a *saqer*?'

'A *saqer* is an evil to its enemies,' she says in Arabic, knowing that she is annoying Zena.

Zena's rage flickers up and then takes over.

'You make everything into nothing or into something else! Everyone goes out with their friends to parties but for you it is a moral crisis. Why can't I have friends here? You are such a hypocrite! You are racist, racist RACIST!'

She storms out, slapping her wet hair against the wall.


'We saw an owl!' Zena's rage is forgotten. Masoud is home.

'God Forbid!' he says in mock concern.

'Why "God Forbid"? It was beautiful!'

'The owl is an image of gloom and evil.'

'Rubbish!' Zena snorts, flaunting her superior knowledge, 'the owl is an image of wisdom and higher learning.'

'Who says?'

'Everyone.'

'I should know what an owl is. I have never heard of this wisdom and learning. At home when we hear of an owl, or see a picture of an owl, we seek the protection of God.'

'That explains a lot Dad. You fear wisdom as if it was death.'

'And you seek disaster as if it was wisdom!' He is so eager for the game that Hiam feels angry.

Hiam is tired.

'It was not an owl, it was a *saqer*.'

'Ah, now the *saqer*.' Masoud can spin stories on words and birds.

But Zena is suddenly bored. The word games are only fun if Hiam laughs.

Masoud retreats into his habitual silence.

The voices crowded in. Memories rose around her like coloured helium balloons, wafted upward on her terrors. She drove on, the land empty of life, deserted, bereft. She struggled to focus only on Zena.

Zena at sixteen. When she turns sixteen Zena suddenly becomes a vegetarian, with no explanation and no exceptions. Hiam feels a shadow creep over her heart. The days of laughter and pride at parties, of adoration and certainty in her daughter, are long gone. They no longer break the same bread, share the same salt. Her daughter, laughing one day in the salt wind on a stormy beach, is gone like a water mark in the sand. She has, in infinitesimal constant, imperceptible, irreversible movements, dug her way out of the known world.

*And now she won't eat my cooking.* There is something hollow about cooking without the loved one eating it. More than hollow, lacerating even.

Hiam becomes masterly with garlic and coriander, marjoram and thyme. Her *lubiyya*, *mnukhiyya*, *kousa* and vine leaves fill the hollowness in her belly for a while. Zena is generous in her praise and her helpings. Most of the Aunties don't understand, but since Hiam is slim, she is able to claim that it is thanks to her relatively vegetarian diet and, since they are all fat, they cannot argue. The battle against fatness and the hope of successful slimming takes precedence over tradition. Nominal vegetarians pop up everywhere.

'Honest to God, Zena *habibti*, they are all vegetarian now. Ilham, Rayya, even Sitt Malika. I nearly became one myself. But you know, they don't go stupid about it. They eat turkey, and chicken, and fish. Won't you try a little bit of sausage? It's mainly bread.'

Then Zena stops eating oil. Stripped of her olive oil, Hiam's heart breaks. She begins to let Zena cook for herself, harrying her, eyeing her for a slip in the resolve, angry, helpless, exiled from her daughter's stomach.

Zena. Hiam glances sideways at Zena, who, noisily eating a Granny Smith, is like a supernatural presence passing through the room. Her daughter: *harsh and inexorable, a palm tree shooting up between us, parting us, discarding us.* She and Masoud are two withered almond husks falling away, dried and meaningless. Their very terrible daughter is no gentle almond sapling. The speed and draught of her passage has something unnatural in it—a new-age monster passing through their lives with a drying, withering *woosh*. Whooping and gasping incomprehensible fragments of an unknowable dialect of English into her mobile phone, Zena floats potently through the room in a studded black bra and walks out the front door. Hiam screams but there is no response. She is alone. She weeps in rage and frustration until she feels dull and desiccated.

She draws parallels between herself and Zena, understanding enough to be impotent, implicated, criminal, paralysed. She remembers the inner satisfaction, almost a joyous peace she obtained by shocking her parents. She never set out to shock them; she stayed on higher, self-righteous, moral ground, revelling in her rightness, her powers, and the irrelevance of their counter-attacks. *She too* walked out the door and off to university with her luxuriant black hair, freshly washed and smelling like almonds, floating aggressively in the balmy breeze, a storm warning flag, a storm yearning flag. She understands Zena. Clothes, whether *hijab* or the black bra from hell, are just clothes. The wearing or the not wearing of them is the action of a self, deliciously, privately alive and powerful. She feels like rending and smashing something, even everything.

Why, she wails aloud to the familiar cornices, could it not have been the same clothes, not different ones? She could have met a familiar clothing rebellion with far greater maturity and wisdom than a strange one. Why could it not have been her own rebellion again, not this shocking, strange someone else's? The stupidity of this makes her laugh. In fact, she liked the *hijab* and only discarded it for a while to demonstrate her unlimited powers. Clutching this fragment of a pattern of experience to interpret her daughter, she tries to comfort herself with wise predictions about Zena's nakedness, at the same time as praying that Zena comes home before Masoud.

It is the fault of a criminal, immoral, cruel country of rapists, prostitutes, neglectful parents and alcohol. Somehow Australians do not love their children as much as is needful and the people are little more than animals. This terrible country is giving the bright, innocent beloved these shocking tools for self creation. As usual she vents her rage upon Australia but in her heart she deadens herself with the thought, *I know nothing about anything except the past elsewhere.*

She wishes (a recurrent daydream) that Zena would stay asleep. She feels exhausted, harried and harassed from the moment Zena wakes to the moment her light goes out. If luminous, smooth, happy Zena slept forever, she would always be in the world of the possible and the ideal, not this actual terror. Implicit perfection and fulfilment, not apparent evolving deviance. She laughs again, bitterly. Do all mothers dream of extinguishing and neutralising beautiful daughters? No, No, No. In reality she wants Zena to become everything and anything, never to stop, never to become tame, never to die, never to wither in unfulfilled dreams and ambitions—wild and free as now. She finds herself thinking that if Masoud were gone—dead, lost, left behind, then she would find it easier to condone and even celebrate Zena's dangerous ascent. She laughs a third time. Her loves are stretched taut, repellent and incompatible. She feels hollow and exhausted by life, of life, with life. She wishes she were single and childless and unassailably free of having to determine, and do, and be seen to do, the right thing. Alone in the house, she stares at the cornices blankly and sobs in desolation.

The world is too cruel here and the Aunties have failed. Ziad beats his wife and drinks but the Aunties have not intervened. Ihsan, Fawzia and Caroline work late in a nightclub, running wild on Hindley Street, and the Aunties are powerless. Samir left home secretly in the middle of the night. Everyone knows that his mother beat him like a carpet every day since he was twelve. Amira is never spoken of by anyone.

Children who were the boast of their parents vanish from sight and are only mentioned strained through smiles and lies. Sometimes they have only moved out of home but a cloud of shame hangs so heavily over the community that every slight anomaly is covered up and wept over. The failed marriage, the mixed marriage: these are the deepest wounds.

The Aunties are all creeping on tiptoe around their own hearts.

She awoke in the tent in the morning light. A memory rose unexpectedly and she clutched at it, rolling it over, savouring it. From a garden cut as a terrace into the slopes she followed her memory out through orange and yellow blooming cacti, with their gay, flat, fleshy hands held in still salute any way they pleased, to the grey stone walls reaching for the sky on the huge, flat rocktop opposite. Rows of little windows, storey above storey, looked out of the façades, every which way too, like the eyes of a friendly dog which nonetheless knows its duty and will not hesitate. At the top of this herd of lovable, enticing stone follies, all on guard, yet leaning together contentedly, were rows of extra large windows, having a startled air granted by their thickly whitened lashes and sills. These their largest windows gave them away. The delight of height, even if it was nine stories shrugging through and leaning upon the neighbouring walls, was winked elaborately and guilelessly from these intricately coloured and patterned *mafraj* windows. The village was built high as high can be, upon the highest, stoniest rock in the high country. Inside these rooms were a multitude of views. One sits in there in the full glory of light, out of breath from the endless stairs, laughing in the cushions and carpets. Capturing the experience of viewing and the view in one. She recalled with a stiffening of surprise and longing, with the tantalising feel of only touching half of it. Frogs all around. Hopping, singing, between the rocks, and orange-winged, crested birds. She began to cry and the potency of the memory faded as she woke up completely. She clung on but could only remember remembering and re-narrated the fragments to herself to pin them down. They fell apart like the ashes of a printed page. The flash of the hot, orange wings of the hoopoe was long gone. Had she stayed and grown there, she might have been happy. It was a happy place. She certainly would not be here having been sucked dry by a man of such ravenous self-pity. She felt stunned. There was such a difference between Masoud as a man and her father and uncles as men. She remembered with a strange feeling like loathing his sobbing face buried in her lap. She felt suddenly horrified that she had allowed him to behave like that. She had, year in, year out, let him touch her with his grieving, clinging, greedy eyes. She had lain there loving him as his rotten stories poured out. She had let him be pitiable and he had not had the strength to love life through her. She had made love to that. She felt rage welling up again. *Masoud, you liar. What could you possibly want out of life that was not right there in your house?* What had happened suddenly struck her as the most dirtying thing she had ever known. She felt an inner disgust that she had ever grieved for him, that she had been shocked at all, that someone so obviously worthless had proved it in such a gesture of self-engrossed suffering. She felt a sudden desire to slap his melancholy face over and over again. *Long-term, self-immolating grief is the most insufferable and unforgivable thing I can think of.* She ached to punch him and pulp him and felt like screaming that she would never get the chance.

The rumble and tumult died away. She was a house whose street wall just collapsed, bombed away, showing all the little tidy boxes of colours and furnishings ridiculous in their mindless neatness and caught out in their pointlessness. What did it matter? She was acutely scarred and exposed and he would never be there to submit to her fury. Why had she never protected herself from this very damaging man?

Was he so dreadful after all?

Masoud eats with theatrical pleasure.

'Zena, isn't our Hiam a supernaturally good cook, a true food poet?'

'Oh yes,' Zena laughs and leans over to her father, popping a large piece of rose scented baklawa into his mouth with her fingers; 'Read this one, aloud!'

'Three stanzas,' he says, 'each more evocative than the last. In sum, it is a hymn to God!'

Hiam laughs,

'Would you like a free gift from the poet?' and kisses him.

His eyes are glowing, piercing, contagious and happy.

'Praise be to God that He has blessed me so!'

She was exhausted. Exhausted with the driving and with the endless land. She had stopped noticing the subtle changes. Change was so unceasing and repetitious that the land seemed changeless. She was exhausted with the screaming descent into her pain and the effort to stave off thinking too much about Masoud.

She dreaded the sideways lurch of the world under her. Each time, her feet and the car would move apart, slowly disconnecting sideways, signifying the descent. Time slowed and seconds passed like hours. She trod the world like a clown on an unstable ball. Everything depended on her. The seconds stretched, their borders encompassing any number of thoughts and feelings, decisions, indecisions and resolutions. Between one kilometre marker and the next passed her whole bundle of memories and shards of possibilities; but without the world rolling smoothly and independently on its course they were meaningless. Terror and boredom mixed. She would wait for things to right themselves, for the seconds to pick up speed, blacking out to endure.

Hiam has become afraid of the stories behind people's conversations. Conversations in the community sting her. The Arabic can no longer soothe. Conversations in the supermarket sting her, especially since her English is now good enough to hear them; conversations in the train, and then at night Zena rubs her raw for the next day of goading and stinging.

Hiam watches Masoud. Life seems so much harder for men. Success is conceived too inflexibly and satisfaction is a very narrow flicker of light in a potentially dark future. Life here could be sufficient for her if Masoud could be happy. Happiness, she tells herself, is a fleeting blessing, not engineered, and never retained, descending in unpredictable moments into a world of sorrow. She herself has never got around to writing her stories down. She had meant to become a writer but that goal was flexible and negotiable. Zena loves and remembers the stories, and will repeat, reinvent and create stories for her own children, never the last in a long succession of storytellers. Hiam has become dependent upon her own words.

She has lost Zena. Zena's marriage was to have transformed the house. With that, life would have again become real. Happy.

Hiam feels robbed. The worst thing is that he is likeable. She had not wanted to see his calm eyes taking her in as well. His silence in the storm of Masoud's pain and rage was warm. He took the prohibitions, recriminations and threats and fears in warm silence. He had *expected* them. She does not want to know that he has feelings. They mustn't matter. He is Australian (well, South African). He is from the world of degraded women, rape, damaged people. He is trying to take her daughter beyond the harmony of her orbit. He cannot do otherwise, since he himself is abandoned in an unnatural world. He is going to destroy Zena and turn her against her parents. Zena has betrayed them to him—he was warm and silent because she has told. Zena has told him Mum is cardboard cardboard cardboard and Father is nothingness.

Later she recalls his odd gaze, holding her eyes. No appeal. Only regard. A regard with no boundaries. She knows that Zena has told him that she loves her mother. Not Loves Mother: I love my mum she's a dear. No, Zena loves Hiam. She feels the hollowness of her familiar confusion sucking her down. *To be torn and torn like this!* Zena always paralyses her, and all Hiam's posturing and shouting are hollow and seem treacherous. She feels sordid. Why could he not have kept his eyes down in shame? He should be so ashamed! Why could he not have come with his parents to ask for Zena, and given Masoud his self-respect and the satisfying, honourable rejection? He did not even mention marriage! He only came to meet them! He was here! In This House! She sits on the edge of the bed with her mouth open in a silent scream and her quivering fingers spread over her lips. She starts to wail despite herself and sits mindless and torn, wailing and staring at the perfume bottle. 'Joy'. She wails until exhausted and sits frozen on the bed as the stars intensify through the drifting curtain. Zena how could you? And in the same moment she knows that the question has no answer and isn't in the right language. The question has no meaning outside her screaming dizzy heart and that makes the scream total. Zena you have betrayed me, deserted me. Why was my world not enough?

The hole in her heart widens and sucks and whirls her and the cardboard Australia into nothingness.

She had to stop the stillness of driving nowhere and began to look for a way off, desperately searching the highway for a break away. Masoud had been hovering just outside the story, waiting and demanding to be told. Her memory veered away from him only to return, hesitant, but ultimately certain. If she let him in, she knew that he would leap up and, with a dizzying rush, shoot straight for the end. Screaming with fear, she would have to wrench herself off his back and cast herself away in freefall. She had delayed long in touching much about Masoud, but he was edging in and, like a pregnant animal, she needed to creep away somewhere quiet and huddle around the pain. As if magically, a dirt turn-off formed itself to the left. It went only a few miles, or so it seemed, before it turned into a two-rut track, and then a little-used path. It lost its vigour: failing, wilting, eventually turned from its once purposeful line by mere tussocks. It wound pointlessly in the expanse. Just as the car began to struggle with the unkempt path, a leaning timber hut appeared off to the left. Hiam nosed the car through the irregular bush up to its side and stopped. It was no more than a kids' cubby, just taller. It was made of stunted, uneven trunks scarcely thicker than sticks, some aged, grey timber slats, and thatched and patched with brushwood tied in clumsy bundles. She stared at it, ridiculously relieved. This was the destination and here she was stopping. It was bleak and deserted but what else was she looking for? She walked in through the leaning doorway and looked around. It was no bigger than a large tent, earthen-floored, dry and dim, with enough cracks and gaps letting in the light to give it a skeletal feel, if not appearance. No-one had been there for a very long time but she didn't mind. She was feverish and thoroughly sick of people and too alone to know herself anymore. She went to the car and carried her bedding, groundsheet and water inside. She made her bed in the middle of the floor and lay down with her head to the east and her feet to the west. She felt very weak and lay until evening, watching the yellowing bands of light from the cracks in the slat wall track up the length of her body.

The house is tinged orange with the dying light, flecked with shadows and bars as the sun sets far beyond the white, tubular steel fence. It is normally a graceless house fronted by an untidy but surprisingly beautiful garden. The front garden is Hiam's and has something of everything she likes in it, grown over the years into something no garden purist would recommend. Mysterious lilies appear and disappear in summer and flowers of intense colours take over in spring. A statue and fountain in the centre of a small circle of lawn is the only similarity her garden has with those of her friends and relatives, many of whom are purists in their own way.

'Let me *help* you with the garden,' Uncle Yusuf

says kindly, almost every time they meet. The different colours of concrete figure heavily in his gardening repertoire. Even brick paving is vastly inferior to concrete, because 'it goes green, and has to be washed with acid.'

The lack of good, tidy, clean concrete in her garden is seen by many to be rather shameful.

'*Ya Haram*, the poor thing. She never *learned* anything: her parents sent her off to university, and she never had time. You know what study is like.'

She eyes the house and garden for effect. Parties are highlights: timeless moments of perfect performance in the deteriorating fabric of their lives. The architraves are lined with little coloured lights which are already winking dimly in the twilight. The glass of the windows shines clear and crystal, giving a view in on a tastefully decorated house, a home full of love and laughter, a good man, good wife, good daughter. It is also spotless: Auntie finger-swipe proof. Looking in on her own house, she also knows that it is in this moment cupboard-peek proof: the silverware drawers and the dining hutch doors are unlocked for anyone who might care to take that hurried, secretive appraisal of another's worth and wifeliness. She looks in, her head cocked slightly to one side like a dog hearing a new sound. She is taking a different angle on this house. It all looks good: modest but decent, and delightful in an indefinable kind of way. Nothing for Masoud to be ashamed of. A taxi driver can still have a lovely life.

Jasmine twines and assists itself up the eaves, scenting the evening air thickly. The fountain plays its music softly, enticingly to the imagined guests. The green lawn is browned and darkened by the reddish light, but nonetheless takes on the appearance of rich glossy velvet. She walks out of the gate and down the street a little way. Then she turns and, constituting herself as a visitor as best she can, walks up to the house to try and catch that first impression. Around the thick branches of the corner conifer and there it is: like a diamond ring sparkling in the twilight. On the deep red roof, a smoky orange cat is respectfully, carefully cleaning itself. She opens the gate, walks up the path, scrutinising the effect. Night falls over the glittering house and, satisfied with its inner and outer presentation, she goes inside feeling contented, even smug. Masoud will see the people seeing his happiness. She has grown to love parties, despite the fact that she always feels angry and exhausted at the end of them. Cleanliness, good food and their education, and their own personal physical beauty is all they have to offer, but it is enough:

'Honest to God, like a movie star: an Arab Robert Redford!'

'Her cooking! *Ya Latif!*'

With respect to Zena, the tired old phrase 'the most beautiful girl in the world' used by countless parents to persuade their all-suspecting sons, simply will not suffice, since she really is shockingly, unprecedentedly beautiful. The blonde-loving Australians stare, look back, wonder. Hiam has seen them.

People come happily to their parties and stay late. It has a lot to do with Zena according to Hiam, to do with Masoud according to Zena, and to do with Hiam according to Masoud. In reality, many members of the community feel as though they are out on a cultural evening. They go partly because being at the Sharifs' makes them feel important, and more Arab without effort. The Sharifs know about things: they know how to tune and play their *'ud*; they read Mahmoud Darwish; they can answer queries on literature; they talk about subjects other than births, marriages, politics, Australians, and gossip about crimes and indiscretions of parenting. They do not have their finger on the weakening pulse of every family.

*Masoud began drinking, quietly, out of sight. He stared red-eyed at the TV on his nights off, eating with no appetite or appreciation. He told bitter and violent stories, and searched out the harsh and violent in history. As he spoke disconnectedly of honour and revenge, Hiam saw his damage and felt more and more helpless. Over time she tried to become impervious to him.*

Everyone has knowledge of something and poetry from somewhere: at the Sharifs' they have their forum for it. Other parties do not bring this out in the community. Other parties tend towards a neighbourhood watch system in which parents exceeding the safe zone are brought into line through degrees of ostracisation and gossip.

At the Sharifs' even children feel they have something to prove and recite their best Arabic, blushing but without shame.

At the Sharifs' being intelligent matters and the poetry learned in the heat of boyhood dreams comes out of the most unexpected people.

Rather than talking about their schooling, their children's schooling, the new bride's degrees and PhDs, here they recite and tell anecdotes. It is a place where some issues lose importance as they walk in through the door and others gain. Masoud's house has slowly become a small but significant cog in the machinery of the community's self-image.

*He no longer slept. He no longer prayed. He repeated only his mother's arguments: Australians are prostitutes, the man worse than the woman. Hiam looked at Masoud and thought: he is being stoned to death like an adulterer from a storybook. He is being stoned to death. He had fallen and could not get up.*

Hiam feels happy. People are ranged about, sitting, gossiping loudly or in hushed tones, joking, teasing, eating and enjoying themselves. Her people, feeling here her love for them and their connection with each other. The gossip is a way of reminding each other and themselves that they belong. Even out here. The food and the community, the voices and the music make them whole, even if it is just for one evening. Knowledge of each other, spread by harsh or gentle gossip, whether cruel lies or compassion, *knowledge and words of me spoken by another mean we are together*. Hiam looks at them and feels a sense of pride at the rubbing, rustling, discordant human whole. Some of the sitting men and women sway and roll their raised hands elegantly, smiling in shared pleasures with their neighbours. Beautiful, slim young women, daughters and new brides, dance, supple and thoughtful but aware, always aware, of the appreciative onlookers. Their mothers and aunties and some uncles dance too. The older women swing and arch their fingers stiffly like the pinions of a bird with the grace and clumsiness of birds, their steps rocking their bulk, shaking and wobbling in a pleasant and proficient way. They dance alone or together, sinking finally into their chairs with deflated gasps and to the clapping from their relatives. She watches them bicker, chide and praise each other and themselves and, as often before, wishes she was not so much an outsider. Harsh gossip about her and Masoud is never said to her face and Zena is only criticised obliquely. However, the dream of every parent (with a few exceptions) is that their children go, as Hiam and Masoud did, to university. And beyond that, Zena is adored.

Evening approached and she tensed fractionally. As night fell she noticed that she was waiting for something. When the moon rose and the cold fell, she knew she was waiting for Masoud, waiting for the sound of his step and his breathing outside the door.

He appeared in the doorway, paused, and then stepped in, crouching in one movement by her side. He picked her up by the neck and held her tightly and kissed her but brought with him no warmth.

'Would you like to hear a story?' he whispered to her softly.

'Yes,' she murmured.

*Once in times long past a prince lived in a magnificent palace with his beautiful sister. Every day the two of them would ride out hunting. On their fastest horses with their fastest hounds and hawks and leopards, they would hunt the creatures which roamed the wild hillsides and desert plains surrounding their city. One day they roused a fleet gazelle, which the prince shot with a well-guided shaft. When they came up alongside her body, they noticed that she was a mother full of milk and, from the discomfort of her full udder, had been unable to outrun them. The huntsmen carried the body back to the palace kitchen, but the princess said, 'Let us look near where we roused her for her young.' They returned along their own tracks to the spot and nearby in the long grasses they found a young*

*gazelle of several weeks, which leaped up upon their
approach and fled. It was, however, inexperienced and
distraught and the best hound soon brought it down. She
pinned the creature, waiting for her master. They stared
at the exquisite, frightened animal and they could not
bring themselves to kill it. Its black eyes stared in fright
at its captors, while the brother and sister looked hesitantly
at one another. The prince then said: 'Let us take her back
with us: we can give her the best of everything in life, and
she can adorn our palace and garden.' Her beauty had got
hold of their hearts, for she was elegant and graceful and
refined, with eyes like the darkest night, and a body of a
rich, gold colour topsides, with a satiny, creamy underside.
Her tail was a plumy flag, with hair like shimmering silk.
The prince himself carried her back to the palace and began
to tame her. After a little while she was so hungry that
she drank the milk they gave her and, because of her
inexperience, tolerated their caresses and affection. The
prince became so attached to her that he insisted she sleep
on a gold-edged carpet next to his bed and every day he
played with her in the garden, tying garlands of flowers
about her neck: roses and anemones, gillyflowers and
jasmine. Every morning they perfumed her with the most
costly attars and on festivals they dressed her in the finest
brocades and embroideries. The princess embroidered a belt
for her brother depicting two gazelles face to face, one in
thread of the purest gold on rich cream satin, and the other
with silver on silk like the moon. The creamy embroidered
gazelle wore a gold, gem-encrusted collar from which
dangled three bugles of sapphire, matching closely the one*

*the real gazelle wore. When the prince sparred in battle play or went to fight in skirmishes, he wore the emblematic belt. He and his sister began to use the word 'gazelle' to mean all things fine and perfect. 'When I find a wife,' he said, 'she must be a gazelle of gazelles.' 'Regardless of our father's and mother's wishes,' she said, 'I will only consent to marry a gazelle.' Meanwhile the gazelle lay by night in the stately chamber of the prince, her fine legs folded under her, her collar and necklaces glittering in the moonlight, her large delicate ears pricked forward, her large eyes shining. In the mornings she ambled on a gold chain behind the two, part of all their games and amusements. They fed her all the delicious things they could order from afar and ate themselves those things she refused: Omani peaches, Shami apples, Egyptian limes, Sultani oranges, Osmani quinces, pistachios, Tihama raisins and all sorts of sweets and confectioneries. In the afternoon she lay between them as they lay under the shade of the rare trees in their garden. They stared at the sky and talked of their future spouses, while she stared out over the high stone wall to the desert.*

*One night, as the gazelle stared out of the window in the dim starlight of a clear spring night, a wafting breeze straight from the desert plains parted the curtains and circled the room, bringing with it a faint smell of the harsh and aromatic sands, the low hardy herbs and the rubbing, rippling muscles of the running gazelles. The gazelle could not contain herself and, thinking the prince asleep, sighed heavily and murmured:*

'Ah! Would that I were running in the wind under the starlight with the gazelles.'

The prince, however, was awake and sat bolt upright on his carpet bed, staring at the gazelle in terror.

'The gazelle spoke. I heard it. The gazelle spoke.' First he whispered it but then, as terror got hold of him, he lost his reason, and screamed in terror:

'The gazelle spoke! I heard the gazelle speak!'

He leapt up and rushed from the room, running straight into the alarmed slaves, his sister, mother and father.

'What is wrong?' they all cried at once but he could only gasp,

'The gazelle spoke!'

He would not return to his chamber, so his sister took him to hers and soothed and nursed him all night, but he could not be calmed. By morning he sank into a deep melancholy and would say very little except the same phrase:

'The gazelle spoke. I heard it.'

He would not return to his room and developed a terror of the gazelle. The king and queen were distraught and had the gazelle thrown into a neglected courtyard in the garden out of sight from the prince's windows. The princess soothed and nursed her brother, murmuring 'I believe you, I believe you,' but this only distressed him more.

'My mind is broken: the gazelle spoke,' was all he could muster in reply. She did not know what else to say, so she stayed by his side, silent. The king and queen sent for all the physicians in the city but all of them were baffled by the prince's illness. They then sent far and wide, offering the hand of the princess as an incentive for the curing of the prince. Physicians from Oman, Cairo, Damascus, San'a and elsewhere flocked to the palace. None of them had ever seen anything like the prince's illness and left disappointed. Physicians from India, China, the land of the Franks and Java arrived but with no better luck.

One day, a bedawi on a fine bay horse presented himself to the chamberlain as a physician. The chamberlain looked him up and down, noting the desert sand still dusting his clothes and the gun slung over his back.

'Are you sure you can heal the prince?' he said suspiciously.

'No,' said the bedawi, 'but I can try.'

The king had given orders to admit any physician, so the chamberlain reluctantly did. The bedawi (a young man with rich black hair and a face like the moon), approached the prince who lay moaning upon his bed.

'Tell me your illness!' he commanded.

The prince looked despairingly and listlessly at the bedawi and merely repeated:

'The gazelle spoke. I heard it.'

The bedawi turned to the king and said,

'Sire, I must see the gazelle.'

Followed by the entire household of the palace, the bedawi was led to the deserted courtyard, which was opened. In the centre of the ruined pavilion stood the gazelle, wearing the shreds and tatters of the hand-embroidered cloth-of-gold pyjama coat made for her by the princess. Her tarnished collar trailed the fine gold chain which had caught in the rusty balustrades of the pavilion steps. She had not been able to reach much food, and had stripped the bark off the trees around her and pulled up the roots of the grasses. She was thin and her hair was dull. The bedawi looked at her in silence, while the king, queen and entourage muttered and shuffled.

'She should have been killed straight away.'

'She is an evil Jinniyya in the body of a gazelle: look at her stare boldly, without fear.'

The bedawi held up his hand and said simply:

'Take me back to the prince.'

Once back in the princess's chamber, the bedawi began to abuse the prince roundly:

'You son of a thousand dogs. Stop snivelling there on the bed. Of course the gazelle spoke.'

There was an outcry from the entourage and the sworder stepped forward waiting for a signal from the king to strike the rude bedawi's head off in one blow. The king however saw an animation and blush on the face of his son which had been missing for many months, and said in a loud voice:

'Silence! Let him speak!'

'Of course the gazelle spoke! Did you listen? What did she say?'

No-one had thought to ask the prince this question and the novelty of the bedawi's method held their attention. The prince stuttered uncertainly:

'She said "Ah! Would that I were running in the wind under the starlight with the gazelles." '

*(The queen gasped in joy and whispered excitedly: 'He said something new!', but was shushed by the king.)*

*'Well why in the name of God does that surprise you? You are not sick at all, merely blind, deaf and stupid.'*

*The prince sat up and looked at the bedawi in astonishment, looked around at the crowd, and leapt up calling for his robe. Then he called loudly for the gazelle and for his sister. The sick gazelle was brought before him and as he and his sister gazed at her emaciated form, staring coat, tatters of finery and into the deep, shining eyes, remorse and sorrow desolated their hearts. With his own hands he began to rip the rags off her body and gently unclasped the collar and chain. Stroking her gently, he dismissed all but the bedawi and his sister. Leading the gazelle with merely a hand at her neck, the three of them walked out beyond the castle walls, over the hills and out into the desert plains. There they released her and, as she leaped away speeding across the sands without looking back, she looked like any gazelle. When they returned to the palace, they were alone: the bedawi had disappeared without asking about the hand of the princess. They could hear the rejoicings from within the castle but they still eyed each other soberly. Then the prince tied on his belt of the embroidered gazelles and they went back inside the palace.*

She woke up sweating under her quilt. The interior of the hut was spangled with dawn dust and patterns of light. She felt lightheaded. She lay still awhile, staring around. Directly above her hung a long swathe of black hair, tied like a horse's tail to the roof beam. It rotated slowly of its own accord and after a little while she recognised her own hair.

She felt no inclination to get up. She lay still, soaking in the steady intensification of the day. After what seemed like hours but might have been minutes, she got up to urinate outside. She squatted, the day glared white hot, the heat sat on her head like a leaden hat. She thought of the world as an oven, with the hut as a little crock-pot, herself the shaken, simmering, conglomerate chunks and juices inside.

Inside, she lay in the same position as before, drinking water now and then from the 20 Litre Water Container with Tap. She knew she was ill but felt quite elated to be ill and not to care. It couldn't matter now that she was ill and in fact illness lessened the pain. Her head hummed with noises and voices: cicadas, herself, Masoud, Zena, Umm Muhsin, Jamila. She knew they were memories and paid little attention.

'MUM, *Mum*, what have you done with my sneakers?'

'Hiam, don't tidy the drawers in the study, I need to know where things are.'

'In my youth a girl, my cousin, was killed for dishonouring the family.'

'*Ya Ibni*, there will be no Jews in Australia.'

'Mum, don't say such rubbish.'

'I don't like the Mosque.'

'Tell me a *good* story. As long as possible.'

'With a face like the full moon, hair like the night, breasts like pomegranates . . . '

'There is a boy at school with a face like the full moon.'

'Glory to God that He has blessed me so.'

'ZZZZZZZZZzzzzzzzzzzzzzZZZZZZZZZZZzzzz zzZZZZZZZZ.'

The voices went on and on, flipping through the themes of her life. She listened with half an ear, concentrating on something else. Deep underneath the cicadas was something else. A steady, unchanging, unceasing hum, almost a distant roar: Masoud's breathing. She concentrated on it fearfully and hopefully, waiting the long wait for moonrise.

At the fall of the cold and the rise of the moon, he came in. He lay down beside her, brushed her unkempt, chopped hair away from her ear, and murmured,

'Would you like to hear a story?'

'Yes.'

*Seven girls of the village dressed themselves up in their best clothes and, taking their baskets, headed off into the wilds to collect Ilb tree fruit. Only the youngest, who came from a very poor family, was wearing old clothes. The others were dressed most beautifully. They came upon an Ilb tree laden with fruit and all stared up, overjoyed. They pressured the oldest to climb up and shake the fruit down, promising to fill her basket with good fruit, not bad ones. She fingered the fine material of her skirt, and protested,*

'If I climb, my mother's new skirt will be torn, and she'll kill me for it.'

The second refused:

'If I climb, my mother's new scarf will get torn, and she'll kill me.'

The third refused:

'My mother's fine hijab will get torn, and she'll kill me.'

The fourth refused:

'My mother's pretty trousers will be ripped, and she'll kill me.'

The fifth refused:

'My mother's necklace will get broken, and she'll kill me.'

The sixth protested:

'My mother's beautiful overshawl will get torn, and she'll kill me.'

They all turned to the seventh and she looked down at her clothes.

'No-one will kill you over those clothes,' they said.

'All right, I'll climb,' she said, although she was afraid of heights. They joyfully shoved her up the tree, promising to fill her basket with good fruit. She climbed high in the tree and shook and threw the fruit down with all her might. Her friends filled their baskets happily but ignored the seventh girl's basket, laughing all the while. When their baskets were full, they started back to the village laughing as the youngest cried out from the tree:

'Help me down! Please help me down! Come back! I cannot climb down by myself!'

*The youngest girl was left alone high in the tree in*
*the wilds, her empty basket and the bad fruit scattered*
*around beneath her. She tucked her feet up under her on*
*the branch and looked down. The evening set in and she*
*began to whimper softly in fear. Then suddenly she saw a*
*man in the distance. She murmured to herself:*

*'God has saved me and sent this man to help me.'*

*The man, who was really a Jarjuf, a jinni of the wilds,*
*came near to the tree and suddenly raised his head:*

'I smell flesh and it's human flesh,

Out of the ordinary, not the usual.

Between my teeth I'll taste it and tear it

I'll rip it and snip it with incisors and molars.'

*The girl looked down at him and said:*

*'A very fine evening to you, O Uncle. I am a little*
*girl stuck in this tree. Please help me down.'*

*'By God, little girl, if it were not for the sweet greeting,*
*I'd have already eaten you, as I am a Jarjuf. I'll let you*
*live. But I have to warn you that behind me comes another*
*Jarjuf, and behind him another, and behind him another,*
*and behind him another, and he is followed by two more*
*of the Jarjufs. If none of them eats you, one of them might*
*help you down.'*

*He left, and shortly after him, another appeared. This*
*second Jarjuf stopped under the tree and also called out:*

'I smell flesh and it's human flesh,

Out of the ordinary, not the usual.

Between my teeth I'll taste it and tear it

I'll rip it and snip it with incisors and molars.'

*The little girl called out:*

'Good evening, dear Uncle Jarjuf. My friends have played a cruel trick on me and left me stranded here. Please be so kind and help me down!'

The second Jarjuf also spared her life, warning and reminding her that five more were to come. He left, and she waited high in the tree.

The same thing happened six times. Each time she greeted the Jarjuf and each time, while he didn't eat her, he didn't help her either.

The seventh Jarjuf stopped under the tree and, as she knew that he was the last, she told him the whole story, after greeting him properly. The Jarjuf considered her closely and said:

'You will have to jump down, and I will catch you, but there are conditions.'

'I agree to them, whatever they are,' the girl said hurriedly.

'I'll tell you anyway,' said the Jarjuf, holding up his hand.

'See this hand? If you fall on the thumb, I will eat you up. Agreed?'

'Agreed!'

'If you fall on the forefinger, I will shove you back up in the tree. Agreed?'

'Agreed!'

'If you fall on the middle finger, I will marry you. Do you understand?'

'Yes, Jarjuf, I understand.'

'If you fall on the fourth, I will kill myself, but if you

fall on the little finger, I will leave you free to go wherever you wish.'

'I agree to the all the conditions,' the girl said.

'Jump then!'

She jumped and fell down down down towards the Jarjuf and the earth. He held up his hand and she fell onto his middle finger.

'According to our agreement, you are now to be my wife.'

'Well and good,' the girl said, 'I am happy to be so.'

The Jarjuf was delighted. He picked her up and flew over the land at an incredible speed. The desert rolled under them as if it was wrapped like paper around a ball. It seemed like no time at all until a splendid palace high on a rocky peak rolled into view and came to a standstill before them. The Jarjuf alighted in front of the gold-studded door and they entered. The Jarjuf rushed through the palace lighting the lamps and calling for food and festivities, while the girl looked around her. Her new husband lived in a most magnificent abode. The floors were of multicoloured marble, the ceilings of gold and lapis lazuli. The alabaster windows were paper thin, and she could see the clouds scudding by through them. The coloured glass windows spread elusive traceries of colour over the polished walls. That night the Jarjuf held a wedding celebration. The palace was lit up until it glowed like a fire on the rocktop. His cousins and brothers and all their people came. All were very beautiful but the girl thought her new husband the most beautiful of all. He had fine dark eyes, fine white teeth, and beautiful, curling lips. She started to lose her fear and began to love him.

'Praise be to God,' she said to herself, 'that he has blessed me so.'

She settled into married life with him in the beautiful palace. Apart from the living and visitors' rooms, the palace had seven great rooms with identical doors. The Jarjuf showed her six of them, all packed with different kinds of treasure: precious stones, gold ornaments, costly brocades and silks and cloths, precious books and scrolls and manuscripts, fantastic armaments and daggers and swords, and carved animals of ivory and ebony and Ud. The seventh room he forbade her from entering and forbade her from looking for the key and made her promise that she would not.

Life continued happily. The Jarjuf treated her with wonderful kindness. She felt blessed indeed. However, as time went by, interest in the seventh room grew on her. The Jarjuf left her to her own devices during the day and she could not stop thinking about the seventh room. One day, stuffed full of curiosity by the Devil, she could withhold no longer. She searched the whole palace until she found the key and without giving herself time to think, thrust it into the seventh door and turned.

She stood in the doorway unable to move, unable to believe her eyes. The room stunk, reeked. The room was packed full of skulls, bones and half-eaten bodyparts. Tossed to one side was a great pile of knuckles and shins. There was a little door at the back by which the Jarjuf entered and left secretly. She closed the door and, shaking in horror, returned the key to its place. When the Jarjuf got home she was clearly not herself.

The Jarjuf was suspicious. He asked her what was the cause of the change and she told him that she was a little bit sick. He was not reassured.

'What happened, did anything happen to you?'

'No, no. I am a little feverish, that is all. I should be better tomorrow, God willing.'

The Jarjuf would not let her out of his sight, while daily she got worse. She thought inwardly about how bad and evil he was, how dangerous. Her life had turned sour and she hated every moment within the beautiful castle. She knew that she could not flee. He was, after all, a Jarjuf, and would most certainly find her.

She became thin and pale and scared of any little movement or noise. The Jarjuf was now certain that she had opened the seventh room. He said to her,

'I see how daily you get worse, not better. I am going to go and get your mother, and see if that cheers you.'

'Can you really just go and get my mother?'

'Nothing simpler,' he said, and flew off. He flew out into the desert and quickly changed himself into the image of her mother, and then rushed back. He knocked on the palace door.

When she saw her mother, the girl cried out joyfully,

'O Mother, welcome, welcome. How are you and Father, and my brother and sister?'

"We lack nothing except for you. How are you? You look so pale, and thin and frightened.

Is he bad to you?

111

Does your husband beat you?

Does he mistreat you?'

*'Oh, no, no. He is wonderfully kind to me. I am very happy. As you can see, I have everything one could wish for.'*

*They chatted warmly together for a while. Then, since it was clear that she was not going to say anything to her mother, the Jarjuf rose and said in the voice of her mother,*

*'Well, my dearest, I must go. I will send your sister to visit straight away.'*

*'Please do, quickly. Farewell, dear sweet Mother.'*

*The Jarjuf flew off into the desert, took his own form back, and flew back home.*

*'Did your mother visit?'*

*'Oh yes. Thank you very much.'*

*The Jarjuf watched her like a hunter at the chase, every minute, every second. She didn't improve, so he suggested to her that he bring one of her friends to visit her.*

*'Can you really do that for me?'*

*'For you, even from the ends of the earth,' he said and flew off into the desert.*

*A short while later her best friend knocked at the door. The girl was overjoyed and the two friends embraced warmly.*

*'You look terrible. How come marriage suits you so badly?*

Is he bad to you?

Does your husband beat you?

Does he mistreat you?'

*'I am so happily married, you wouldn't believe it. I*

112

*am just a little ill right now. Nothing at all to worry about.'*

*They chatted a long while. The girl praised her beautiful husband, his kindness and generosity, and the six rooms of beautiful things he had given her, and her friend congratulated her warmly. The Jarjuf (for of course it was the Jarjuf) soon realised that his wife was not going to say anything about the seventh room to her friends, so as soon as he could, he excused himself and left, promising to visit again. He changed himself into her sister.*

*When she saw her sister at the door, she burst into tears and rushed into her arms. She held her a long while, until her sister said,*

*'Sister, dearest sister, what is the matter?*

Is he bad to you?

Does your husband beat you?

Does he mistreat you?'

*'No no no. He is sweet and kind. He has given me everything one could ever wish for. There is just one thing that is upsetting me.' And she told her all about the seventh room. Then she said,*

*'Now I hate my life. He is a Jarjuf and he eats people, and I cannot forget it. I cannot sleep because I see their bones and I am so sad that I think I cannot live.'*

*Her sister, who was of course really the Jarjuf, held her tight and said, 'Yes, he is a Jarjuf, but as you said he is good to you and kind to you. You should try to see the good in him and love him as you did before.'*

*Her sister left and the girl tried to think about her words. But the sadness had crept into her bones and she*

113

got thinner and thinner. The Jarjuf watched her like a hawk, from near and from afar. He didn't know what to do next, now that he knew that she knew.

One day she was walking amongst the rocks on the high plateau, wondering what to do about her unhappiness, when she saw a young goatherd in the distance. She called him over to her. He neared and she was astonished to recognise her sister, disguised. They fell into each other's arms in joy.

'O my sister, what are you doing here?'

'Sister, dearest sister, we have been looking for you far and wide for months and months, ever since you disappeared while picking Ilb tree fruit!'

She stared in horror and, as her sister told her tale, she realised what the Jarjuf had done. She told her sister everything that had happened. Her sister in turn insisted on returning together to the palace to take care of her.

There was no point hiding. The Jarjuf came home and immediately began:

'I smell flesh and it's human flesh,

Out of the ordinary, not the usual . . . '

His wife didn't let him finish. 'Yes, here is my beloved sister, come to visit us!'

The Jarjuf made his sister-in-law most welcome, realising at the same time that he had been discovered. He thought of eating both of them on the spot but then decided to wait and see what his wife would do. He waited two days, until he sensed that his wife was relaxing and believing in his apparent friendship with her sister. Then he suggested,

'How about I and your sister go to the souq together and do some shopping?'

'Yes, and God go with you.'

The Jarjuf took his sister-in-law into the desert, drew a knife and cut her throat. Then he chopped her up into pieces. Some meat he ate then and there on the spot and the rest he put in his basket to take back home. On his way a hawk circled above him, flew down and snatched a finger from the basket. The hawk flew over the palace and dropped the finger, which had her sister's ring still on it, into the girl's lap. She realised at once that her sister had been killed.

Just then the Jarjuf arrived home.

'Your sister left me in the souq, saying that she wanted to return home straight away. She sends her greetings. Take this meat and cook us something nice for dinner.'

Hiding her grief, the girl took the meat and cooked it and served it to him.

'Why don't you eat? Come and eat with me!' he said.

'Truly, I am already full. Too full to eat!'

He ate, drank deeply and slept. The girl collected all the bones together with all the leftovers and put them with the finger and the ring. She took them out into the garden and buried them in a small grave.

She watered the grave every day and before long a tree seedling appeared. It rapidly became a sapling, then a small tree. One day it had a huge flower bud upon it, which she picked. In her room it opened and a perfectly formed little baby girl emerged. She was the very image of the girl's dead sister.

When the Jarjuf got home he said straight away:

'I smell flesh and it's human flesh,

Out of the ordinary, not the usual.

Between my teeth I'll taste it and tear it

I'll rip it and snip it with incisors and molars.'

'There is no-one here except you, and me, and this new-born baby!'

The Jarjuf was beside himself with joy that he had a daughter and celebrated extensively. He provided anything and everything for the small, growing child. He almost stopped watching his wife but not quite.

When the child had grown to be a beautiful young woman, intelligent and wise beyond her years, strong and skilled in all the arts of sword and horse, her sister–mother told her the whole story.

'The Jarjuf loves you as his daughter but you are indeed my beloved sister whom he killed and whose flesh he made me cook and whom he ate.'

She incited her sister to revenge her death and to rescue her from the Jarjuf.

'Fear him no longer, dear sister. Together we will free ourselves from him.'

'Then listen to my plan, for there is only one thing to do, and that is to kill him. And there is only one way to kill him. The Jarjuf can only be killed with his own sword. As you know, he goes to sleep early. Tonight, you too go to bed early. I will retire to our room and he will follow. He will lay his head in my lap and sleep. You must find his sword, draw it carefully so as not to make a sound and come quietly into the room. Beware. If the Jarjuf's eyes are open, he is deep asleep. If, however, they are closed, he is still awake. Wait outside the door and I will signal to you when he sleeps. If his eyes close while you are in the room you must be very still until they reopen. You must strike him once only with the sword. Remember, it must be once only. Pay no attention to anything he says.'

They waited until nightfall. After dinner everything went as planned. When the Jarjuf saw his daughter and wife retire, he too felt sleepy and went and laid himself down with his head on his wife's lap. For a while he lay with his eyes closed but then they slowly opened. The sisters exchanged secret signals and the young girl entered soundlessly, carrying the Jarjuf's own sword. She raised it and brought it down hard enough on his neck to sever his head from his body without cutting her sister's legs.

The Jarjuf cried out,

'Once more! Once more!'

The girl remembered her sister's advice and replied:

'My mother taught me
Neither to leave the dough unbaked, nor to bake it twice!'

'Kick me with your foot!' cried out the Jarjuf.

'My legs are too short!'

'Just spit upon me a little!'

'My mouth is too dry!'

The Jarjuf died and the two sisters left him where he lay. They rushed from the palace carrying some of the

117

*treasure and headed out across the wild desert towards home.*

She woke up breathing hard, looking straight up at her gyrating hair. Her chest was stinging. She was naked under the quilt and pouring with sweat. She was crushed with thirst and sat up to reach for her glass. The stinging sensation became acute and she looked at her chest and breasts in surprise. They were crisscrossed with lacerations, some of them quite deep. Her chest and stomach were covered in trickles of coagulated blood. She fingered the wounds, struggling briefly with her memory, but giving up. She drank deeply and washed her chest a little, and lay down, passing the day in semi-consciousness, listening for the dim sound of Masoud's breathing.

It had changed. It muttered and spluttered rhythmically, constantly, sometimes fast, sometimes slow. The other voices had faded to whispers, dry shaken leaves of no consequence. She listened with concentration:

*Chyse Chokka Chyse Chaw Chyse Chokka Chyse Chaw Chyse Chokka Chyse Chaw Chyse Chokka Chyse Chaw Chyse Chokka Chyse Chaw Chyse Chokka Chyse Chaw Chyse Chokka Chyse Chaw,*

until she could hear him breathing loudly outside the rickety door.

At moonrise he came in and lay down, cupping her stinging breast, stroking her chest. He kissed her nipples and, raising his beautiful head, looked her in the eyes and said softly,

'Would you like to hear a story?'

'Yes.'

*Completely pale, shaking, Zena played the last unanswerable card,*

*'What makes you think I am still a virgin?' She shrieked at them, engulfing them in the hurricane of her fury and frustration.*

*The room changed. Masoud shuddered with a long, shaking, involuntary movement which brought him to his feet. His daughter stared at him, her eyes wide and tortured. Hiam's gaze tracked slowly around to Masoud. Darkness was falling outside and she could only see the shadows and rifts marking out the contours of his face. Her throat was dry and strained and she suddenly realised that it was she who was screaming. She stared at Masoud, avoiding the shaking form of the girl.*

*Zena felt exhilarated with the sensation of freefall before striking the earth. The only way was to give them nothing to fight for and she would just weather the abuse they would have to heap on her. Her mother was still screaming and gasping. Zena looked at her for a moment and hated her. Her screaming was horrible, cloying, obscene.*

*Hiam began sobbing in fear, staring at Masoud's silhouette in the window.*

*Zena shook with the desire to strike her mother down. Why couldn't she have a boring little talk about the pill, like a normal mother? Why did Zena have to be responsible for her parents' happiness? She clenched her fists at her sides and, without knowing that she would, shut her eyes and began shouting hoarsely,*

*'Stop it stop it stop it. I didn't mean to tell you like this. Why must you be like this? Why can't you ever be happy? I love Rudiger and he loves me. We are going to . . . '*

*The words of her love fell hollowly, meaningless in that room. She felt protective of her love and ashamed of it. Shame was the felt, or the done, shown in the wrong place. She looked at her father: a solid black cut-out of a man rigid in the window. She had expected him to threaten murder, to shake her, to shout and storm about. She wished he would, because she was sure he needed to and she was ready for it. She eyed him worriedly, feeling spent and empty-hearted. She longed for the warmth and peace and the chance to cry, curled up in Digger's arms. She was starving hungry. Her father was motionless as stone by the window and her mother was sobbing strangely, staring at him. She felt for a moment that they had forgotten her presence. Her mother was afraid and Zena suddenly became very very frightened, panic rising through her, straining every filament. She could hear her father breathing, sounding stiff and dry, like paper, and something else: it sounded as though he was smiling. She wanted to run away. The room was full of strangeness and her parents made no sense. She was so exhausted with them. It was going to be good to force them to be a little independent.*

*Hiam's mind strung a few thoughts together experimentally and then gave up.* The girl—she would beg forgiveness. I hope she knows how to feel guilty. No respect for her parents—shame upon the family—a good family, but she chooses to be a prostitute—we gave her everything—Australian madness. *They were other people's words, other people's thoughts. They were the decoy from the implosion at the heart of it. Zena had left them, bringing an* intifada *into a momentary and decisive encounter.* Masoud Masoud Masoud—what will you do?—turn to me, please move, melt, scream, cry with me.

*A voice came out of the shadows which Zena couldn't recognise.*

'Leave. Leave now.'

*It was a command from somewhere far away and she obeyed. Outside the front door of the house she hesitated. Should she really leave when things were so strange and unresolved? She looked at the familiar doorstep and didn't know how to step back over it. What could she say? If something so not his business hurt him, what could she ever say? What was there to say now?*

*A flicker of rage tugged at her idly. They only loved the virgin in her. She was literally a stranger to them for having loved Digger as love and nature commanded that she do. They had lost their real love for her and loved only their image. Shame and honour in the eyes of the community were far more important than their daughter's happiness. This was the old, old story and she toyed with the phrases half-heartedly. Having told them, she couldn't feel the same battle fervour. She knew they loved her: just right now they had lost the Muslim parents' vocabulary of love. She began to sob and ran down the road, past the corner, past the bus stop, past the deli, past the station, past the dark casuarina park and into a long gumtree-lined avenue leading beyond her suburb. How far to Digger's? Digger, Rudiger, please help me. Everything has happened and is more awful than we imagined.*

*Hiam rushed out after Zena but it was too late. The child was gone. She would come back. Where was Masoud? She went inside. He was still there, standing behind the desk. She thought she better do something for him, so she raced to the kitchen and shakily made coffee—quickly, quickly—she was shaking all over. What would he say? The mother is always to blame. She knew that he knew that she was to blame. She had never had the heart to make Zena be good. She had spun her web but she hadn't believed in it.*

*There was a loud sound from the study. Was that just now or was she remembering it? An unplaceable, impossible sound in her head. She stood still, listening. She must have imagined it. The mirror must have fallen. She dropped the coffee and ran. She slipped and fell at the door, got up, and ran softly, softly, until she pushed the study door open. Masoud was gone from the window. She walked out. Coffee. Yes. She drifted away, dimly conscious of the fresh air. The hall didn't smell.*

*Smell. She turned and, crossing the hall in two strides, flicked the light on in the study. She leapt the desk in one bound, descending like a cat on the other side. Between her legs was Masoud, his head to one side with a silently widening halo of blood. An acrid smell; and a sweet, moist,* raw smell. He had been shot. Someone's gun was still there on the floor. She sat down astride his body and stared at him. *Ya Zena, your father loves you. Ya Zena, habibti, he has left us without thinking. Ya Zena, kiss your father for me. Ya Zena, Zena, aiyuni, he is with you. Zena, Zena, Zena, he didn't mean to hurt you.*

His face was white and blue and red and black. Blue shadows, white skin, red blood, black hair. Eyes closed, a gentle mouth. He looked like Zena when she was young, once, when she had cried herself to sleep. She thought: *When did I last kiss him? Passionately, deeply, longingly? Years. When did we last make love together? Months. When did we last laugh together? Weeks. When did it all end? Just now.* She opened her mouth and squeaked, and hit him lightly. *Masoud—none of this meant this. None of it at all.*

She felt dizzy. There was a rushing and roaring in her head. She got up, walked out, shut the door, went to the kitchen and made another coffee. She put it on a tray, with a saucer over the beaker, put two small cups on the tray with two cakes, and walked to the bedroom and set it down on the dresser. She sat down on the bed and waited a moment. Then she called Masoud softly. He was outside in the garden. She listened to him putting the shovel down, scraping his shoes off at the doorstep, shutting the door. He creaked through the house, sounding each of its noises, coming towards the bedroom door, familiar hiss of fabric against the walls, familiar click of the light switch, familiar footsteps. She scratched her hand. It was sticky. She looked down in the dim gloom and saw a thick black crevasse, *dividing her hand in two. She touched it to her tongue. It was blood. The footsteps stopped at the door but he didn't come in. She had heard him breathing but now he was holding his breath, for hours and hours and hours.*

She awoke gasping, feeling as though she was drowning. It was dawn and she was drenched all over, shivering in the sodden quilt. She wondered if she was lying in her own blood, weak because bleeding. She was thirsty and freezing. The 20 Litre Water Container was on the wrong side of the bed and was completely empty. Her water was gone and she thought without panic that it had significance; she would most certainly die today. The sun was rising.

She could smell something. A smell had been in her nostrils from the moment she awoke. It had slowly flooded her mind and now took over her thoughts. Acrid, intensifying, familiar from sometime long ago. Not quite water on a heated stove. Water. Her water was gone and it had rained. She and Masoud had watered the world. It reeked like coriander and black pepper pounded in a mortar, harsh and sweet. She knew she was smelling the earth, reeking, rising, swelling, stretching the wonderful soil. A rough, raw, rank joy tolled in her mind, recalling a high, modulating song too loved to be heard without pain. The call to prayer.

*Allahu Akbar.*

She got up, turning her damp body in the dawn light to dry. She dressed and went outside into the shimmering day. She kneeled with the sunlight on her right shoulder and self-consciously prayed a ragged prayer, with her face to the spicy earth, smelling the wet soil.

When she stood up she was weeping. She felt hollow and sad but quite sane.

She was alone. She had been alone for days, weeks, months. She was experiencing a strange world and the worst loss possible utterly alone. She felt as though she were being cored out from the inside. Where would she return to? Who would she ever tell the story to? Masoud was gone and never again would look at her, impressed, amused, astounded. She had been so unbelievably brave but no-one would ever know and even if they did, it would not reach her excoriated inner self. Who was she if no-one knew her? The sense of loss of Masoud was compounded by the sense that with his departure her self had been dragged away screaming. What could it mean to be beautiful, intelligent, gifted, spectacular, alone. *I am like a book fading out of sight under the ocean or in desert sands. What do I say, if I am forever unread?* Masoud was dead and she was truly alone. She felt beyond hollow. She felt the transfixing horror of an intense physical impalement. From her bottom to her brain the wrenching of her aloneness and nothingness yanked her rigid back into the seat. She howled as never before, roaring motionless at the wheel of the speeding car. It could not be abated. *I am not nothing: I am unalloyed pain.* She began to gasp,

'Help me help me help me help me help me Oh God help me.' She whispered and then fell silent and drove on blankly, guarding the physical pain in her centre.

The road floated under the car. It was a road from nowhere going nowhere and she was merely crawling upon it for something to do. She was walking in the desert in the wind scuffing up the sand at her feet. The wind suddenly whipped up skeins and swirls of sand around her, enshrouding her in a pale red cloak and obscuring her vision. She held down the folds of the cloak with her hands and peered through. A man was walking towards her through the sandstorm. She gathered her cloak around her and waited. He came up to her and the instant she saw his eyes, she recognised him. She froze in something between joy and fear. The Blessed Prophet Muhammad looked at her closely, and said,

'Who are you?'

'The mother of Zena.'

He looked more closely.

'Who are you?'

She said uncertainly,

'I am the wife of Mas'oud al-Sharif.'

He stared into her eyes, and said gently,

'Who are you?'

'I am lost.'

'God bless you and take care of you, Hiam,' he said and, as he turned and disappeared into the desert, the wind rose around her in a high howl, ripping her cloak and the sand away. A road train shook her car off the shoulder of the road, its screaming horn trailing mournfully away behind her. Maybe she was going somewhere and it didn't matter that she didn't know. She drove on. *God is the All-knowing.*

*There is no God but God, and Mohammad is His prophet.*


She walked into the service station and bought some food and Sprite, some car oil and asked for her water to be filled. She liked the rough friendliness of the man carrying her things for her.

'Where's ya car?' She pointed to the taxi.

'You caught a *taxi*, lady?'

'No. My husband used to be a taxi driver.' Driving out late. Cleaning the car so that each customer could believe that they were the first to vomit there. Soiling the taxicab: $50.

'Used to be? Why don't ya take that thing off then?'

She had never thought of it. She looked at the car and thought that an Adelaide taxi looked pathetic, exiled, out here. She wondered how it was attached, that little slavish cap. She thought of chopping it off with an axe, chiselling it off, flattening it, setting it alight. Probably it had screws.

'Could I borrow a flathead and a Phillips head, please?' She hoped she didn't sound too odd.

'I'll take it off for ya,' he said kindly, and did.

The car didn't look the same. It wasn't the same car; it was renewed, nobler, more fitting. She had not realised how out of place it was until it was fixed. She tidied the inside a little and wiped some red dust off the dash. She pulled out self-consciously onto the highway, making her grand entrance.

She walked along a hot and dusty pavement, coffee in her hand. She wasn't sure where to go to drink it. She was a stranger, a drifter, and her indecisiveness welled up. She faltered and stopped, unsure if she even wanted to drink the coffee at all. She suddenly became aware that she had stopped in front of a man with a brown paper bag of groceries leaning against the wall in the shadows under the awning. He looked almost Sudanese. She felt confused and embarrassed and said softly without thinking,

'*As-Salam 'aleykum.*'

He smiled at her, and said wonderingly, laughingly,

'Oh Yeah—waleykum Salam!'

She was so startled that he laughed. She stuttered,

'Do you speak Arabic?' He shook his head.

'Nah nah. An old fella taught me that when I was a kid.'

A woman in a red T-shirt came out of the shop and stood beside him. Their two bodies accommodated each other in the small shade and they formed as much a single picture as if they were embracing.

Hiam wavered. She didn't know what to say next but she felt an urge to prolong the moment. She held out her hand awkwardly and said,

'My name is Hiam Sherif.' It was the first time she had dropped Sherriff but she still pronounced it the English way. She shook first his hand and then the woman's hand.

He said, 'I'm Noah, and this is my wife Annie.' Annie smiled. Hiam couldn't walk away and blushed because she still couldn't find something to say.

'You alone?' Annie said suddenly. 'How about you come along have breakfast with us, then.'

Noah and Annie lived in a small cottage away from the great, dividing road. They had a small, very shy daughter who was hungry enough to stay in sight only as long as it took to get food. Toast and jam and gentle rough people, and hospitality. Hiam wanted to cry but she talked instead.

'Yeah, you've had a hard time, Mrs Sherif. You take it easy. Travel some more. The Green North— she's gonna fix things for anybody.'

'Why is it called Tennant Creek?'

'Coz in the dry,—not even enough water for ten ants!'

'Really!?'

'Nah!—I dunno why she's called Tennant Creek!' And they all laughed, even the child behind the wall.

Noah had never heard of Islam. But he was a little curious and kindly. He had heard of oil and knew about camels.

Hiam had never heard of the Gagadju or the great storms of the Top-end. She had heard of crocodiles and she could see that he was homesick for his family somewhere further North in the green paradise of his childhood and that he only worked in Tennant Creek. Annie laughed and struck him lightly now and then, punctuating some private story.

It was after midday and hot like a furnace when she was again on the endless road, rushing into the humming, chaotic rhythm, vibrating in the geometric division of the vanishing road. The deep red earth divided in two even halves to let her pass. Noah's 'And upon you Peace' still reverberated in her ears. The crucible of the land was closing over her like the closing of a hand. And upon you be Peace.

Somewhere after Mataranka Springs Hiam thought of Zena. She turned completely white and felt the cold sweat leap fear-driven from her pores. Staring ahead and seeing nothing, she thought of Zena. What had she done? She had spent days, weeks barely thinking about Zena, only remembering her. She felt sick with guilt. Why had she thought nothing at all about Zena? Why had she simply driven away with a few picture memories and the ghost of Masoud? She pulled over and ran from the car, bent double in physical pain. She stood in the tussocks a little way off the road, her ragged hair hanging in the wan, young moonlight. Her bare feet sank a little into the still warm, blood-black sand. She felt tears drop one by one onto the skin of her shadowy feet. Zena. She didn't think of a rape scene, a death scene, a murder scene, a graveyard scene. She thought suddenly of the last time she saw her, the only time she had seen her *after*. Zena had appeared out of the darkness in Muhsin's back garden and had stopped still in front of her. Hiam stared at her in shock, seeing the thin figure, the jeans, the hair gone, cut short, the eyes. Zena had opened her mouth to speak but in a swift movement had leaned over the garden bench, kissed her softly, and fled. Holding on to the image with effort, Hiam scrutinised it. Zena in the garden, not an apparition, not a dream. She had smelled Zena's breath and she had smelled unwell. She had a very similar memory of Masoud in the same garden but she knew that the one of Masoud was a dream or delusion. *Masoud is dead and Zena is under this same moon and sky as I, at this very moment.* She almost thought of what Zena must be feeling but her mind veered away from the possibility of that encounter and she rocked her head to chase it away. She moaned softly in the intensifying moonlight. She sensed Zena's ribcage swelling with each breath she took. She thought of Zena's tears running as she licked at the corner of her own mouth. Her living breathing daughter filled her mind and body and she started to sob with longing. Her loneliness took her breath away but it felt sane and clean.

The call to prayer rang out:

*Allahu Akbar. Allahu Akbar.*
*Ashhadu an la Illaha illa Allah*
*Ashhadu an Muhammadan rasul Ullah*
*Hayya 'ala as-Salah.*

She was scrambling over the multicoloured rocks of the *wadi* of Bayt Baus. Her playmates were long gone and she was alone. She could not make it home in time. The dry silt of the *wadi* floor clung to her legs as she struggled and stumbled over the rocks. Her hands rummaged ineffectually for a hold on the glittering red and green pebbles, trying to avoid the sharp diamond-like crystals in amongst them. The *wadi* curved unnaturally, unusually. It became more and more serpentine. She struggled to run but could make no headway. The *wadi* floor was moving slightly under her. Her scarf was wound tightly about her hair but somehow still it loosened and fluttered to the ground. Its beautiful white folds began to sink and disappear under the pebbles and silt, which were jostling one another as if something were passing by underneath them. She turned and tried frantically to loosen it from the *wadi* bed. It was an 'Eid present from her father, the most beautiful and important thing she owned. She started to cry. The call was over, and the sermon had begun. She was too far away to hear it clearly. She started to clear away the sand and pebbles where the scarf had disappeared. The *wadi* floor was moving and the last layer of stones would not budge. They were fixed in place like great textured scales. She thought suddenly of praying here, on the *wadi*'s back. There is no need to get home to pray, she told herself. She felt very relieved. She was kneeling with her palms flat against the scales. She crooked her thumbs under them, held on, and began to recite, moving rapidly now through an unfamiliar valley.

She knew that this was definitely the Green North, the vanguard of the Green. Green had crept into the picture silently, insistently, with straggling grasses and palms, filling and flooding the world. Everything was green. The car was still dewy, silent and still. She was drinking coffee, her feet on the dashboard. She looked northwards through the windshield, feeling happy. Beyond the dashboard, between her bare toes she could make out a stand of green fans, waving palm trees. Green Australia. She stretched her toes, heels resting on the dash, and tried to place a single tree between each two toes. She could not focus on her toes and on the trees, so she flicked back and forth to line them up. Sprouting from each gully was a dim and magnificent palm tree. It was irreconcilable; either toes or trees. Keeping them carefully lined up, she stared at the sky through the window against her right shoulder. It was breakfast-time, time to wash, time to go, time to greet the reassurance of the highway. A car passed, marking the trail noisily. She froze for a second to save the palm garden and then leapt out of the car. 'You are mad, Hiam. No people and no purpose.' She felt a wave of accomplishment. The land was truly green.

She thought of the tyre monsters in the pink lake and began to laugh. Someone had actually made them just to be seen, to be a joke glimpsed while passing on the highway. The crocodile was becoming her excuse and had as much or as little reason or meaning.

'Well, I decided to see what crocodiles were like.' Why? 'They are wild and free like me.' She was not immune to the absurdity of this but the impenetrable nature of the joke soothed her. Don't ask why it's pink, she told herself. Because . . . the tyre monster! This had a logic which could only be clear to her but she had a strong sense of taking part in an arcane sport: weaving meaning out of nothingness for one's own purposes.

My husband killed himself, so I went to find a crocodile. It was very funny and she couldn't stop laughing every time she repeated it to herself. True and absurd. Her own story, mapped out in blood on a line on the ground leading to a crocodile.

She reached a city which ended at the shores of a sea. Maybe it was an ocean. It lay to the north, not the south, of a green green green city. She thought fuzzily that she had passed over the infinite land to the other side. This could not reduce the infinity of the land for it rang on, strumming an endless chord in her body. This other side was something else, something achieved by entering into the land, perhaps a mental state only. The highway vibrated harmoniously, unceasingly in her head, something which both could never have been and could never have ended. The car meandered crazily, dreamily down to the whispering shore and stopped. She got out, took off her shoes and, staggering as if her legs had forgotten how to function, made it to the water's edge. It was a calm grey water, salty. Truly it was the sea. The sand was soft and fluffy, like whipped egg whites. The shells were unfamiliar white spirals, lying about like discarded horns of unicorns. She stared out at the horizon, wondering how to think about being at this point without eroding the fragile sense of achievement. She tried not to ask many of her old questions: *what can it mean anyway, to have crossed a foreign land. What can it mean to have felt and thought all that alone. What can it mean except madness to have experienced madnesses. The drive, the direction, all madness.* She struggled only partially successfully to suppress all and tried to think only: I am Hiam who crossed Australia alone. She was Hiam who mapped her torture with a land and a car. She had not expected all this of herself. The soft grey wavelets rustled at her feet, whispering in breathless rushes.

She looked down at her sinking toes and murmured aloud her own name. The water rustled, whispered, muttered, sighing through the syllables of the other word, the land's name. She thought vaguely of swimming but sat down on the sand instead. She stared at the fronds of the trees to her right. They were like great green hands or paws stroking the sky; green, sinuous, ribbed and reptilian. She thought of Noah and Annie in their hot dusty sunlight. A father and a mother. This was indeed the Green North. She would see a crocodile. She touched the whispering fringe of the water once more and walked back to the car. She drove to the nearest service station and asked the attendant.

'You could check out the croc farm here in Darwin.'

She thought awhile. This was unexpected.

'I would like to see a Gagadju crocodile.'

The boy looked at her closely, with very black, shining eyes. He seemed to her strange and beautiful. She wondered if he too was named after a prophet.

'Gagadju? South Alligator, ma'am.'

This was startlingly cryptic. She suddenly felt nervous. She decided not to ask him his name. He produced a map and, leaning against the car, pinned it with one elbow to the roof edge and flattened the rest out with a beautiful, long-fingered hand. He began to show her the intricate traceries of the land she had entered. She looked sideways at his slim, wiry body. He was wearing a loose, faded, green sleeveless singlet over pink shorts and sandals. Every line of his young body showed perfect grace. Every line of his neck and shoulders was painfully beautiful. She wondered if she could remember such a form. She thought of Zena. She could understand if Zena looked at this boy and loved him. Her eye wandered over his neck, his ornate ear, his brow, his shining eye. She bent to look at what he was showing her, overflowing with love for him.

South Alligator River was along, not down. She didn't have to go southwards, just east. It abounded in crocodiles and you could go out in tin boats to see them and to catch fish. They were wild and free and dangerous. If you got into the water you were

' . . . dead for sure, ma'am.'

It would take a couple of hours to get there.

She rang Muhsin. She could not remember when she had last rung him. She had a strong urge to talk and talk to tell him quickly quickly all she had achieved and who she had become. The horror, the discovery, the hut and the Green North. As the number was whispering through its self-verification, sounding like a crazy insect voice muttering in her ear, she realised dully that only to her was her madness real. None of it could mean anything. Not to Muhsin. She thought of him, placing him mentally as a study of worry, careworn in his living room, with his family, worrying about his crazy, grief-struck sister-in-law, grieving too. She made him begin to cry. She felt her panic storm approaching and, hair on end, felt the familiar rush of sickening sweat leap out all over her body. He answered. She told him calmly and briefly that all was well.

'Did you say *Darwin*!?'

She felt an intense pleasure at the tone of his voice.

She also wrote to Zena. As the pen touched the paper she felt a wave of happiness. She again had to master the urge to pour out her experiences. She suddenly hoped that Zena was with Rudiger, comforted and helped by someone who knew and saw her.

It was all too real. After the phone call and after the postcard, she thought shakily that all this, this green world of the unseen animal was real only to her and only now. *Oh, God is Great, Zena, God is Great.*

She smiled uncertainly at the beautiful attendant as she got into the car. He smiled back, catching her eyes and holding them in a kind of embrace, his black eyes warm, encouraging, polite, confident that she was off to do as he had directed. It was a hero's farewell and it was also a simple matter. She smiled again, gratefully, and drove off. She named him Ibrahim, despite the fact that it was clear from his name tag that he was called Dave.

She had chanted softly to herself as she climbed the steep sides of the cliff to reach the waterfall:

*In the name of God the Compassionate the Merciful*
*Praise be to God, Lord of the Worlds . . .*

She was sitting on the flat rock beside the source pool holding her open hand in the water. The water flowed inexhaustible and clear between her fingers. Then it settled, rolled, rippled infinitesimally and gently spilled and fell smoothly over the broad lip, its whisper building to a roar not far out of sight, dividing in an unending shout to columns, ropes, threads, drops and drifting mist. It danced its seamless measure without speed or hesitation. Her face was drenched from the drifting spray.

*'Lord of the two Easts, and Lord of the two Wests*
*Which of your Lord's blessings would you deny?'*

**THE SPOTTED SKIN**
Rowena Ivers

*Shortlisted for* The Australian/*Vogel Literary Award*

When Cressida discovers that she has the curse—leprosy—she is incarcerated on a remote and barren island. In tropical rains and blistering heat, far from home and family, the island's occupants confront appalling conditions and the constant threat of disfigurement and death. And, despite brewing racial tension, they are also redeemed by searing moments of compassion and understanding.

An unforgettable novel about identity and prejudice.

ISBN 1 86448 766 6

From the *Sydney Morning Herald*'s Best Young Australian Novelists, 1997 and 1998

THE BLINDMAN'S HAT
Bernard Cohen

*Winner of* The Australian/*Vogel Literary Award*

'So, you can bring the trumpeters out now. Let the red carpet roll. Open the door of the limousine and let Bernard Cohen step out. Watch the flashbulbs pop. Here is an *Australian*/Vogel Literary Award winner who fully deserves the gong.'
*The Australian*

A crime pastiche with themes of love, neurosis, paranoia and 'the American way'. Genres pop up and are pushed back down again as *The Blindman's Hat* reveals itself in a distinctly filmic manner. There's the grand romance of Vernon, the expatriate journalist, and Dida, a mobile telephone technician, meeting in the park; there's the trail of red herrings and crossed wires that they stumble across and there's even a touch of Lassie in Muffy the dog's loyal antics.

ISBN 1 86448 316 4

## MORE GOOD BOOKS FROM ALLEN & UNWIN

From the *Sydney Morning Herald*'s Best Young Australian
Novelists, 1997 and 1998

**SNOWDOME**
Bernard Cohen

'Bernard Cohen's latest novel, *Snowdome*, may be the single
most brilliant work of intellectual fiction to have emerged from
Australia in recent years.' *Courier-Mail*

It is the present. William and his friends live in Sydney, a
mumbling city. They think about the future, and thinking hurts.

It is the future. Sydney has been emptied out by economic
forces and re-opened as a museum. The museum guide's task
is to describe the city's history to tourists but he can no longer
tell if that history is true or if he has made it up.

'Bernard Cohen's deadpan style is spiked with humour and
wit. This novel blends a hip sensibility with a more enduring
seriousness, a kind of compact Perec.' Tom Flood

ISBN 1 86448 690 2

From the *Sydney Morning Herald*'s Best Young Australian Novelists, 1998

CANDY
Luke Davies

'*There is only heroin, there is only Candy, the three of us adrift on the endless sea of love.*'

*Candy* is a love story. It is also a harrowing investigation of the raw heart of addiction; its claustrophobia and momentum. From the heady narcissism of the narrator's first days with his new lover, Candy, and the relative innocence of their shared habit, *Candy* charts their decline. Davies is a very fine writer and *Candy* is confronting, painful, sexy, tender and at times darkly hilarious.

'a powerful debut . . . you will not forget *Candy*.'
*The Australian*

ISBN 1 86448 339 3

From the *Sydney Morning Herald*'s Best Young Australian Novelists, 1998

**CAPITAL, VOLUME ONE**
Anthony Macris

*Shortlisted for the Best First Novel in the 1998 Commonwealth Writers' Prize*

'Given this volume, we eagerly await the next.' *Courier-Mail*

'The most assured and interesting first novel I have encountered for years.' Don Anderson

Anthony Macris takes the reader on an unforgettable journey through the overcrowded tube tunnels of London and the sparse, sprawling suburbs of Brisbane. Macris's dry, penetrating humour sheds a wry light on the ironies and paradoxes of everyday life and his writing of contemporary urban life is a vibrant and extraordinarily original depiction of a world that seems to be collapsing under the weight of its own cleverness as it splinters and surges into the next millennium.

ISBN 1 86448 298 2